D0895702

THE RETURN OF SILVER CHIEF

THE RETURN OF
SILVER CHIEF

By JACK O'BRIEN

Illustrated by KURT WIESE

THE JOHN C. WINSTON COMPANY

PHILADELPHIA

TORONTO

OTHER BOOKS BY JACK O'BRIEN

CONTENTS

LIST OF ILLUSTRATIONS

I

"PROCEED TO CAMERON!"

SERGEANT JIM THORNE of the Royal Canadian Mounted Police stood outside his home and watched the postman become a small, distant object against a brilliant January background of blue skies and snowy fields. The next moment he turned to the pile of letters in his hand and began to shuffle them. At the third, a familiar, long, official envelope, he paused and exclaimed, "So it's come at last!" Then, noticing the postmark—Aklavik—the Mounty whistled in surprise and tore open the flap.

1

The short whistle made Silver Chief, the great gray dog beside him, prick up his ears and await a further signal to action. For once his master paid him no attention: Thorne was too deeply concerned with the contents of the letter. Signed by the District Chief Inspector at Aklavik was one brief message. It read: "Proceed at once to Cameron River Post to patrol district."

Jim Thorne's brows knotted in a frown. He could not believe his own eyes. A second, then a third time he read the sentence. Of all the things he had expected Headquarters to write him, another job in the Hudson's Bay country had been furthest from his mind.

For several months he had been here at home in the Laurentians with his wife, Frances, and their boy, Donald, enjoying his first real vacation in years. In the last affair with the murderer Laval, Thorne had been badly burned, and the medical chief at Headquarters had ordered him to take a long period for rest and recovery. Here in the peaceful hills above a small lake, the hard, exciting life of the man hunt had seemed far away, and for a time he had felt no great desire to return to it.

Old-timers had warned him often that nobody could keep up the strenuous pace of the Mounted

Police for many years. Then, too, airplanes were now being used in the North to do many of the important errands once left to Huskies and a sledge. This was a good time, Jim felt, for him to retire from the Force and enter civilian life, where two or three worthwhile positions had already been offered him. On jobs where a Government officer with a dog team was still needed, some young fellow, he argued to himself, could take over Jim Thorne's share of adventure.

As his strength returned, he had felt less satisfied about his plan for the future. All the world was at war, and Canadians everywhere were volunteering for service overseas. Each day Jim realized more clearly that he could not settle down comfortably at home while other men fought and died for freedom. Finally reaching a decision, he had written to Headquarters asking permission to retire from the Royal Canadian Mounted Police and enlist in the Army.

That had been a month ago. Until today no answer of any sort had come to the letter, and this note did not even mention his request. Without one word of explanation, he was being ordered out on a routine police assignment in the Hudson's Bay district. Puzzled, Thorne frowned again. He had never been given a job with so little information about what was to be done. Ordinarily, simple patrol duty was assigned new recruits. There must be real trouble of some sort around Cameron, otherwise the "Old Man," as the Chief Inspector at Aklavik was known to his subordinates, would not have asked for someone with a sergeant's rank and experience to cover it. In that case, why weren't there more details? Well, there would probably be plenty of them awaiting him in the mail at Cameron.

Slowly Jim turned to the dog beside him. "Chief," he said, "it looks as if we're going to take the trail again. I suppose the Government knows better than I do where a man can be of most use."

As if understanding this speech, Silver Chief straightened and made a soft, rumbling sound in his throat. Smiling, his master thumped him on the back, and they started up the slope to the house.

"There's one thing about this job, old fellow," Jim continued, "we'll work together. In the Army I'd have had to leave you behind, and you wouldn't have liked that one bit."

Two days later Sergeant Jim Thorne and the Chief were speeding on an express train across Canada toward their new destination north-west.

Thorne was by nature a man of action. When a case was assigned to him, all he asked for were a few cold facts. With these clear in his mind, he went straight ahead and let nothing interfere with the job in hand. This unswerving determination in the face of hardship and difficulty had gained him rank and reputation on a force famous all over the world for courage and achievement.

Had the Chief Inspector sent him to Cameron for the definite purpose of tracking down a dangerous criminal, Jim would have started off without a worry; instead he was uneasy. On the trail puzzling complications merely challenged his wits, but when a job began as blindly as this one, it bothered him. Had he guessed that it was to prove one of the most baffling of his career, he would have felt much worse than he did.

The small trading post on the bank of the Cameron River bore the same name as the waterway. This settlement consisted of the store and about twenty cabins. In winter, half of these, belonging to trappers out working their lines, were closed. So were three others, two of which had been deserted by their owners and one that was always held in readiness for Government Police use. The rest of the log houses were occupied by families of married men.

Late in the spring each year a number of Indians pitched tepees on the outskirts of the community and remained there until fall for the business of exchanging skins, meat, and fish for store supplies and equipment.

The trading-post building was the largest; and the lean and lanky trader, Bill MacDonald, the most important man in a good many miles. His store was crowded with foodstuffs, camping equipment, guns, harness, traps, and rope—all the usual merchandise to be found in a northern outpost. One small partitioned room with a stoutly padlocked door held a small pile of skins. These had been brought in early by trappers needing emergency supplies. By summer when all the winter's catch would have been exchanged, this small room would become a temporary storehouse for fur treasure worth its weight in gold.

The Post was the center of other activities. Here mail was loaded and unloaded by the visiting postal sledge. Men who came in after hard, lonely weeks of living in the bush made straight for the store, as hungry for the companionship to be found there as wolves for food in midwinter. When talk grew dull, the small radio in the corner furnished entertainment. The set, which was for both receiving and sending purposes, gave the listeners the feeling of being closely linked with the outside world that otherwise was so far distant.

With MacDonald lived Danny Hughes, veteran of a thousand winter treks. Danny had long since slogged his last mile beside a swaying dog sledge, but his mind continued to dwell in the vigorous past when he had roamed Canada's Northwest Territory. The old man considered himself an authority on everything which had to do with this district and never failed to express opinions freely. He and MacDonald argued all of the time, but the two were close friends and would not have known how to get along without each other. Like most men of his time, Danny had spent money freely and saved little for later years. Around the Trading Post, though, there were plenty of chores, and the old fellow independently earned his keep by doing these.

One January afternoon as dark was falling, a heavily loaded sledge drove up to the store. The driver jumped from the runners and, hurrying into the building, asked Bill MacDonald, "Is there a doctor anywhere around here?"

Surprised, the trader shook his head. "Doc

Wallace won't be comin' from Aklavik on rou-
tine inspection for another month or so. Far as
I know, there's nobody else in a hundred miles."
Then he added, "What's the matter?"

Giving his name as Frank Blaine, with a mining claim about thirty miles to the southwest, the
stranger explained that he was on the way to
Aklavik with his wife and child to catch a
steamer bound "outside." The day before on the
trail the wife had been taken sick and was now
much worse. Since she could not stand traveling the remaining sixty miles to Aklavik,
he wondered if they could find shelter here.

In the frozen North men grow hard in the bitter, unending struggle to outwit the weather and
make a living. Yet nobody can be kinder or more
generous when others meet with misfortune. This
was true of the Cameron people with the Blaine
family. At once an empty cabin was opened,
heated, and the sick woman put to bed. The few
women in the village took turns nursing, but in
spite of all that they could do Mrs. Blaine died the
following day.

By noon a week or so after the funeral, Jim
Thorne, driving the last lap of the journey by
dog team, arrived in Cameron. He was given a

By noon Jim Thorne arrived in Cameron.

hearty welcome by the group of men hugging the stove in the store. Bill MacDonald and Danny Hughes had been the Mounty's friends for years, and from previous assignments in this district he had become acquainted with a number of others.

"What wind blew you in here, Sergeant?" Hughes asked in greeting.

Flinging aside his parka, Thorne answered with a grin, "I just came down a little early for the summer season in this resort."

A weather-beaten Scotsman chuckled, then inquired drily, "An' which hotel are ye patronizin', Officer?"

"The same as usual if it's not too crowded."

Since this referred to the closed Government cabin, the group guffawed. "Nae, ye'll no find it o'ercrowded," continued the Scot, "I can promise ye that!"

"Goin' to be with us a little while, Jim?" MacDonald questioned.

Thorne nodded. "Long enough to make some routine patrols. Have you had a quiet winter down this way?" he asked between puffs on a cigarette.

"Quietest in years," Mac replied. "Weather's

been so bad nobody's had a chance to get into mischief."

"The North ain't what it used to be, Sergeant," Danny Hughes broke in. "In my time it took more'n weather to keep a man from blowin' the lid off once in a while."

"Don't expect a policeman to complain when things are quiet, Danny," Jim replied. "We're not so fond of work as that." Turning to MacDonald he added casually, "Got some letters for me?"

"Not a thing, Jim," said the trader, "but the mail's due again the end of the week."

Although taken back by this reply, Thorne gave no sign. Instead, he answered a number of questions about the war and other things of general interest. Later when he went out to his team, one of the men exclaimed, "That's a fine-looking lead dog you've got there, Officer."

"You're danged right it is," exploded Danny. "That's the best dog in the Northwest," and with that he was off on a long tale about Silver Chief's history and adventures.

Thorne smiled at the old man's enthusiasm and drove off toward the cabin he was to occupy. Finding no word from the Chief Inspector had disturbed him. Well, perhaps there hadn't been time for it to get there, and Andrews, the postman, would bring something along the end of the week. Until then he would have to be satisfied to settle down quietly in Cameron.

II

A STRANGE AGREEMENT

THAT same night, as Thorne stood over the stove in the police cabin, cooking his evening meal, Silver Chief rose, bristling, from his place on the floor and growled ominously. Jim listened in silence, and almost at once there was a knock on the door.

"Come in!" the Mounty called.

The heavy log door swung in slowly and a stranger appeared. "You're Sergeant Thorne, they tell me," he began.

When Jim nodded, the other went on, "I'm Frank Blaine, and I've come to ask a favor."

Thorne pushed the food back on the stove to keep it warm. "Sit down," he invited. "Now what is it?"

With few words, Blaine told of his recent loss. Then he went on, "I've decided, Officer, not to head for Aklavik. I never did want to go outside—that was my wife's idea. Now that she's gone, I plan to go back to my claim. I'd have started before this if it hadn't been for the girl. She's just eight, and I can't have her with me in winter, for there's nobody to keep a fire going in the house while I work." He paused and Thorne waited, wondering what was coming next. "When I heard this afternoon that you were going to be in this cabin for a while," Blaine went on, "I wondered if you'd let her stay here with you, Sergeant."

Jim stared at him. People often made peculiar requests of the Mounted Police, but this was as strange as any he had ever heard. His first impulse was to refuse. Then he thought, probably the poor fellow's so upset by his wife's death he doesn't realize what he's asking. Blaine was in a bad spot, sure enough. He had no doubt already tried to get one of the Cameron housewives to look after the little girl and been turned down.

The few women in places like this were mostly half-breeds who were always overworked, and whose small, rough cabins were crowded to the limit by their own families. On the other hand, to expect a policeman to tie himself down to such a job certainly took nerve.

"How long?" Jim questioned abruptly.

"Depends on how long you'll be here, Officer."

"My time's always uncertain."

"If I could have until it warms up in spring— say in May," Blaine went on slowly, as if in thought he were already back working the claim.

A silence followed. Then the Mounty said flatly, "I'll have to think it over until tomorrow."

Blaine thanked him, said good-night, and left. Alone, Jim served his food and ate slowly. Ever since his arrival he had been busy with chores: cleaning and heating the cabin, storing supplies, and looking after his team. Now all he wanted was to get this food inside him, fall into his bunk, and sleep. Tonight he was too tired to bother himself with Frank Blaine's queer proposition. The first thing after breakfast he would slip over to Mac's and check up on this stranger.

It was almost noon the next day before he sought out the cabin where Blaine and his daugh-

ter were staying. There he got a real surprise:
Frank Blaine might be only a rough prospector,
but watching his child, who was named Patricia,
Thorne realized that the dead mother must have
been very different. Against the cruel background of the North the little girl looked helpless
and out of place. Dark curls framed the soft
childish face like a velvet cap, and her large
brown eyes glanced up shyly and seriously into
Jim's own.

Without a word from his master, Silver Chief
walked over to Pat, as her father called her, and
sniffed gently. The next minute the child was run-
ing her small fingers through the dog's thick coat.
In that instant they became friends, and if Jim
had needed any further persuasion, he now had it.

Turning to the father, he said, "I suppose you
know you're asking a lot, but I'll give it a try
until April, if I'm still here. No later, mind you,
so remember to be back on time. If I have to leave
before then, I'll get word to you somehow."

Before nightfall small Pat Blaine was comfortably settled in the police cabin. She made no great
fuss about her father's departure, except to stand
for a time at the window looking wistfully after
him. The lonely little figure tugged at Jim's heart.
In an effort to make her forget the parting he

called, "Pat, what do you think of having your room in this corner?"

For the next hour Jim busied himself putting up low shelves and hooks for Patricia to use in washing and dressing. When her few things had been neatly placed, he hung a blanket over the opening, then set about preparing food.

Young as she was, Pat had been taught to be helpful. She carried things to the table, helped stack the dishes, and after playing with the dog, went to bed.

Afterwards Thorne lit his pipe and wrote a letter to his wife, telling her that he and the Chief were now temporary guardians of one small girl. He could imagine Frances smiling over this arrangement, for she had a warm heart for strays and outcasts; she would probably want him to bring the youngster home with him when his job was finished.

Silver Chief rose suddenly, stretched, and rubbed against his master's knee. Jim turned and scratched him between the ears. "Old boy," he said with a grin, "I don't know just what I've let us in for this time, but I suppose you and I can handle it together."

In the weeks that followed this proved true. Thorne had no reason to regret that he had promised to look after Pat Blaine. She caused him little extra work, and having her to think about helped to take his mind off the puzzle presented by this job. Now that both father and mother were gone, the child turned her affections to "Sergeant Jim," as she called him, and Silver Chief. The dog was very gentle with her, and they promptly became close companions. Soon Cameron grew accustomed to the unusual sight of a pretty little girl and a powerful sledge dog running up and down the narrow trenchlike paths and tumbling in the drifts.

As MacDonald had predicted, the postman came again at the end of Thorne's first week in the Post, but brought no mail from Aklavik for the Mounty. Jim sat down immediately, wrote a long letter to the Chief Inspector, and sent it off by return post.

Since he could not hope to hear from this until the next mail, he made in the meantime two short patrol trips of a day each. These resulted in nothing of interest, and when an answer arrived at last from the Old Man, Jim was more bewildered than ever. This communication gave him to understand that the Chief Inspector could supply few definite instructions at present. For the time being, Thorne was expected to see that everything was in order in the district and to keep his eyes open for any strange or suspicious happenings.

Jim studied this letter gravely. He had the uncanny feeling that the Old Man was trying to give him information that he dared not put on paper. There was something very peculiar about the whole Cameron affair. If, for instance, the Chief Inspector could not give one of his own experienced men a clue to a situation, what was going on at Headquarters? Was somebody higher up running this show down here? Since Canada's declaration of war, Government Intelligence and the Royal Canadian Mounted had been working together. Perhaps this quiet backwoods section was the scene of something so important that the matter could not be discussed safely either by mail or wireless. If that were the case, why hadn't the Old Man asked him to run up to Aklavik, only sixty miles away? Covering the district with no idea what trouble to look for might turn out to be a real job, far more difficult than the original order had led him to believe. In police work things had a way of breaking loose when least expected, and whatever it was that faced him, Thorne made up his mind not to be caught napping if he could avoid it.

III

THE STORM'S SECRET

DOWN from the Polar Sea the north wind
pounded, driving frozen needles of snow
against the Trading Post. As if furious at being
denied entrance, the gale tore at doors, windows,
and chimney pots, but without success. The stout
log store had been built to withstand Arctic
storms, and the three occupants, MacDonald,
Danny, and Thorne, were too familiar with bliz-
zards to pay this one special attention. Only Silver Chief, stretched full-length on the floor,

seemed to listen carefully to each shrieking, terrifying blast.

A crackling fire painted the big iron stove cherry-red, and an oil lamp suspended from a rafter swayed with each impact of wind on the walls. This spread a warm glow over the center of the room and cast grotesque shadows into the farther corners.

Sitting on the counter that ran the length of the room, Bill MacDonald swung his long legs and drew thoughtfully at an evil-smelling pipe. Across from him, Jim relaxed in the only comfortable chair and felt thankful that he was not on the trail tonight bucking this storm. Hughes stood with back to the stove and soaked heat into his gnarled old frame, much as a parched field drinks in a shower, while he argued with MacDonald.

Recently one of the Cameron trappers had lost his lead dog and bought a new one. "Tom says he's the best Husky he's ever driven," Mac had just remarked, and that set Danny off as usual.

"He howls too much! No Husky worth his weight in harness is noisy."

"Watched this one work yet?" Bill asked.

"Don't have to! Anybody knows a good work dog hasn't breath to waste. When he does, he ain't workin'!"

The trader stuffed more tobacco into his pipe bowl with a thumb the color of a walnut. Lighting up, he questioned between puffs, "What about timber dogs? They're good workers, yet I've heard them howl plenty."

"We—ell," the older man admitted grudgingly, "timber dogs are like men. They get so lonesome in the woods they have to talk to themselves. What's more, they've wolves for neighbors, an' you know well as I do, when dogs hear a wolf pack, they answer back. It's the wild strain in 'em comin' to the surface."

By this time Danny's back had become uncomfortably warm and he turned to face the stove. Stooping, he rubbed his knees, and the glow from the fire made his wrinkled cheeks look like worn brown leather.

After a moment of silence he went on, "Trouble these days is there's too much playin' and pettin' goin' on—ruin any dog—even the best. A Husky's got to be one or the other, pet or worker—it just ain't in him to be both."

MacDonald's eyes twinkled. Exchanging mischievous glances with Jim, he exclaimed mockingly, "And you say that, man, in the same room with Silver Chief!"

At the sound of his name, the dog's ears

twitched. He rose with a noiseless grace that belied the power in shoulders and flanks, and moved to Thorne's chair. There, pressing a cold muzzle against his master's outstretched hand, he looked up inquiringly.

For a few seconds the three men eyed the animal, then Danny retorted, "You ought to have better sense than to think Silver Chief's any proof, Mac. He ain't a real Husky to begin with, and Thorne knows a lot about handlin' dogs. I'm talkin' about the ordinary variety of sledge dog."

Jim entered the argument for the first time. "Danny, Mac's just trying to get under your skin. He knows most Huskies can't stand very much petting, but they all like some of it. It's been my experience that the way a dog acts tells a good deal about how he's been treated. Give the average sufficient food and a little kindness and he'll work until he drops. Beat and starve and overwork him, and before long he's mean and vicious as they come. For all that the Chief's part wolf, attention has never seemed to spoil him." He rose and stretched. "I think I'll go home and turn in. Pat's in the cabin alone, and if she's not asleep this gale may scare her a bit."

"Mebbe you're right, Jim, but I doubt it. Seems to me she's got a good deal of nerve for a little

The dog moved to Thorne's chair.

tyke," replied MacDonald. "You might expect a young 'un left like her would carry on a lot."

"It's good she doesn't," Thorne said, drawing on parka and mitts, "since she's having to look out for herself early in life." Then he added slowly, "Soon as this storm blows itself out, I plan to hit the trail again on patrol duty. This time I may be gone several days. Danny, would you mind looking after the fire at the cabin and sleeping there at nights?"

"Why don't you bring her over to stay with us?" MacDonald interrupted. "If you're goin' for several days, she'll be better off here. Danny already thinks he's her guardian Number Two. Next thing you know he'll be stumpin' the province telling people how to raise children."

Danny snorted at this speech. "Of course, Mr. MacDonald, ye're not the least interested. That picter book you sent for is for the Chief here to read, I s'pose, or are you buyin' it for me, perhaps?"

Listening, Jim Thorne laughed and said, "Well, thanks for the offer anyway. It takes a load off my mind." Then adding a cheerful "So long," he went out into the night, with the dog at his heels. In that moment of opened door a flurry of snow pushed in and the flakes scampered madly across the floor. MacDonald sat still and watched these melt in the heat.

The fire was Danny's chore, and the old man now shook the grate and began to stuff the stove with solid chunks, to last until morning. "Thorne's a good chap," he said suddenly, adjusting drafts, then slapping dust from his hands. "There ain't many men would've been willin' to help Blaine the way he's doin'. What keeps me guessin' is why they sent him down here now."

"Search me!" replied the trader. "I don't believe Jim himself really knows. Of course the police always have to keep some things secret, but Jim don't go round makin' mysteries out of nothing, and certainly not with old friends. Yet he acted queer when I sounded him out the other day. Said the Inspector at Aklavik had simply told him to patrol the Cameron District for a while. That might mean fur stealing or anything."

"Fur stealing? Think we wouldn't have heard something about that?" broke in Hughes. "Did you ever know a trapper to keep quiet about a robbed line?"

"Not after the first skin disappeared," Mac said dryly, then went on, "I have a feelin' somehow this job's bigger'n fur stealing."

"Well, there ain't no other trouble a man can

get into down here except a fight, and I ain't heard
o' nobody bein' murdered."

"That's what I keep tellin' myself," Mac replied,
"but Headquarters didn't send one of the best
Mounties in the force down here to play ring-
around-a-rosy." He yawned. "The only thing to
do is wait and see."

Hughes sat down and began unlacing his moccasins. "Any way you look at it," he said after
a moment, "Frank Blaine ought to be thankful."

"Yep! Lucky thing for him and for little Pat,
too. Nobody can be tougher than Jim on a man
hunt, but he's sure got a soft spot for children
and dogs. You know," he added, moving toward
their sleeping quarters at the rear, "I've never
been able to figure out how Blaine could go off
and leave the little girl here with strangers.
Maybe losing his wife that way upset the fellow
more'n we thought." Undressing, the trader
crawled in between blankets. "Come on to bed,
you old fossil," he said in a lighter tone, "and if
you start snoring tonight I'm goin' to toss you
out on your ear."

"Wouldn't mind lettin' me know ahead of time,
would you?" Hughes jeered. Then returning to
their previous talk, he said, "Mister, if you ask
me, Blaine worried more about his claim than

anything else. Talkin' about the place bein' rich as Klondike or Kirkland Lake! Told me he'd never have left it if his wife hadn't kept tormentin' him about the child needin' playmates and schoolin'. If ever I saw a man with 'prospecting fever,' it's Frank Blaine, and when that gets a good grip on you, nothing else matters," he finished.

In another five minutes both men were sound asleep.

Meanwhile Thorne and Silver Chief had pushed for a hundred yards or so through blinding snow to the police cabin, and entered. While Jim threw off outer garments, the dog moved over to a bunk at the side of the room and gently prodded its occupant with his nose. Satisfied that all was well there, he then dropped to his haunches and stretched out in comfort.

His master lifted the lid from the stove and added fresh wood. At once the log chunks crackled into bright flame. The open draft door spotlighted the bunk where Pat lay sound asleep in a nest of deerskins. Glancing at the small flushed face, Jim felt a wave of pity sweep over him. The thought of his own child in such a situation as hers made him shiver, and Donald, a rough and ready boy, was much better fitted to meet hardships than this youngster.

Quietly the man turned away, finished attending to the fire and went to bed. Sometime in the future, he determined, when there was nothing more important to do, he would look up that mining claim of Blaine's and see for himself whether it was worth anything. If Pat were to have any kind of decent life, it seemed likely that somebody beside her father might have to keep an eye on her. His last thought as sleep overtook him was a hope that the storm would wear itself out tonight and permit him to start on patrol duty after tomorrow.

On the floor Silver Chief dozed in comfort, his brain alert to every unusual sound in the dark world of wind, snow, and sleet just outside the cabin. In dogs, hearing is many times keener than in man, and scent far sharper than hearing. The great wolf-dog's senses were particularly strong, but even his were handicapped now by distance, storm noises, and the familiar odors of the closed, heated cabin. Outside on a clear, quiet night, scent or instinct might have conquered distance for him and led the animal to explore the river bank farther down. Had he done so, the missing piece to the jigsaw puzzle that was Jim Thorne's present job might have been found at once and saved both master and dog a long and painful chase.

IV

SILVER CHIEF LOCKS A CLUE
IN MEMORY

DURING the night the storm blew itself out, and when Thorne arose the gray sky gave promise of clearing later. After opening the fire and starting breakfast to cook, he caught up a shovel and, with Silver Chief at his heels, stepped out on the small cabin porch. Then he dug through a high-banked snow to the shed and looked after the eight team dogs.

When he re-entered the cabin, the Chief dashed in beside him, and running over to Pat's bunk, nudged her with his muzzle. Drowsily the child ignored this signal for rising.

Snuggling down under the cover, she begged, "Go 'way, Chief! Go 'way!"

The dog, who had first learned this game with Jim's son, gave his victim no peace. When she made no move to get up, he caught the slippery deerskin in his teeth and pulled it to the floor. The next minute Pat, exposed to the cold room, tumbled out of bed.

"Good morning, young lady," called Thorne in greeting. "Get your basin and I'll give you some warm water."

Yawning, and rubbing sleepy eyes, the little figure obeyed. Then she carried the filled basin carefully back to her special corner of the room.

"Is it still snowing, Sergeant Jim?" she called out while dressing.

"No, but it's too cold to play outside this morning. Perhaps by noon the weather'll warm up a little. Now come get some of this hot porridge and bacon in you!"

When breakfast was finished, he said, "My first job is to dig us out. The postman's due and he'll spend the night here with us."

At once the child's face lighted eagerly. "Will he bring me a letter from my father?"

"I can't promise that, but I have a feeling," he went on mysteriously, "that Soapy will have something or other for you."

"But there's nobody else to send me anything."

"You just wait and see!"

The child seemed lost in puzzled thought, and Thorne told himself that if Frank Blaine didn't write his lonely little girl somebody ought to wring the fellow's neck. Well, there would be a package for her, at least, for Jim had given Andrews money on the last trip to pick up a toy or a doll in Aklavik.

" 'Soapy' is a very funny name," Pat said suddenly.

Jim smiled. "He got that when he was young and a bull cook over at the mines at Great Bear Lake."

The child looked interested but puzzled, and the Mounty explained. "A bull cook, Pat, helps the head cook peel potatoes, set table, and wash dishes. When Andrews did the dishes, he used more soap than water. The men soon nicknamed him 'Soapy,' and it's stuck to him ever since. He wasn't much good in the cookhouse, but the North doesn't have a better postman."

After lunch, when the mail had still not come, the officer began to wish that he had not raised the child's hopes ahead of time. Each day, in order to keep his team in top condition, Jim harnessed them to the sledge and gave them a routine run of about two miles and back. Since he was starting on a journey in the morning, there was no need for that this afternoon, and he had plenty of work here to keep him busy. Pat loved these rides, though, and it might take her mind off the mail if he let her go alone.

"Pat," he suggested suddenly, "now it's warmed up a bit, how would you like to exercise Silver Chief for me?"

"You mean me and the Chief all alone, Sergeant Jim?" she asked in surprise.

"Just you two! Get your things on while I harness him."

A few minutes later, bundled in furs, the little girl sat on the sledge.

"Remember what I've taught you about driving, and don't stay long," the Mounty counseled.

She caught up the reins. Struggling to make her childish voice sound as deep as a man's, she cracked the whip in the air and ordered to Jim's amusement, "Mush, Chief! Hike! Mush!" With one slight tug at the harness, the dog pushed forward across the white expanse of snowy plain.

After watching them for a moment, Thorne turned and went into the cabin. There he began to sort supplies and equipment for his trip. By half-past two the packing was well under way. In another hour darkness would close in on this frozen world. Going outside to the shed where meat was stored, he chopped off great chunks of frozen venison and fed the other team dogs their evening meal.

Meanwhile Pat and Silver Chief reached the end of their regular run and came to a halt. At once the dog dropped in his tracks to rest. After a few minutes he looked back at his small mistress for the word to turn homeward. The next instant the hair along his backbone stiffened. He rose, strained forward, and sniffed.

"Lie down, Chief!" the child ordered. She was thoroughly enjoying this first experience at driving alone, and had no wish to hasten its end. Snuggling down in the fur robes, she began to plan what she would do tomorrow when Sergeant Jim left and she went to stay at the store.

The dog had paid no attention to her command. The air was teasing his nostrils with a scent unusual to this lonely place without a cabin in sight.

He rose, strained forward, and sniffed.

For the moment he could find no answer to the puzzle, and, until he did, the animal, with every sense alert, would continue standing ready for action.

About two hundred yards away the half-frozen men who had buried themselves in snow for warmth did not realize that the dog already sensed their presence. Their first thought on the sledge's arrival was that the man they had bribed to help them had finally returned. When the sledge stopped and the driver sat still, this hope began to fade. They were weak from hunger and exposure, and with every passing minute the desire to sleep became harder to fight. This newest disappointment seemed unbearable.

There a short distance away was a sledge, a Husky, and warm furs. To each of the desperate men, it seemed to offer salvation. Could the driver be persuaded to help, as that other had done who found them in the storm? Or would they have to kill him to keep him from raising an alarm? From this spot he did not look very large, but the way people up here bundled in furs made it hard to guess size accurately. If they had to shoot him, that might cause trouble when the other man returned. But suppose the other did not return?

Suppose he did not think the rest of the money worth the risk of finding them food and shelter? If he stayed away long enough, they would freeze to death, then he could return and help himself to what they had.

Trying to save breath, they discussed the matter in short, painful whispers. Swiftly they reached agreement on three things: this was too good an opportunity to lose; they would approach the driver together; later they would decide which one of them should benefit from the affair. With an almost superhuman effort they began to dig themselves out of the snow.

During the next two or three minutes that had passed while the hidden men thought and planned, Silver Chief had not once relaxed. To the strange scent had been added the sound of men's voices. He stared in their direction and suddenly saw a figure crawl out of the snow. The figure rose slowly to its feet and, after a time, was joined by another. They began to stagger forward.

In all the routine runs to this place, the dog had never met a man. To have men crawl from snow seemed even stranger than the first fact. He longed for his master, for some sixth sense warned him of danger. At such times it was his custom to stand and fight. Had Thorne been present, he would have released the Chief from harness and together they would have faced these men. Today, though, the dog felt weighed down by responsibility. The child had been trusted to his care and she must be returned safely to the cabin. Some instinct said, "Go home! Go home! Go home!"

Lost in her own thoughts, Pat had neither heard nor seen the strangers. When she had finished the subject of what to do at Uncle Mac's store, she began to mumble all the terms used in driving a team. This would be a good time to try them all on the Chief and find out how good a driver she was. Her small gloved hand caught up the whip. Before she could crack it in the air, or give an order, Silver Chief swung the sledge around and dashed in the direction of home.

This unexpected start almost upset the passenger. Regaining her breath, she managed to call, "Whoa, Chief, whoa!"

For once the animal did not obey. Having caught the sound of a shot from the rear, he merely increased speed. Behind him the frustrated men watched the prize on which they had laid such hopes disappear from view, and saved their remaining bullets. Now they were tortured by a new fear. The driver had seen them and raced off to give the alarm. Unless their helper returned at once, they were doomed for certain. They had no way of knowing that the driver was not a man, but a small eight-year-old girl, nor that the dog and not the driver had decided when to leave.

When Silver Chief raced up to the police cabin, the spruces, which at midday were blackly silhouetted against the gray sky, had now begun to merge into the gloomy background. Rosy with cold and completely ignorant of the peril she had just escaped, the child called out excitedly, "Sergeant Jim, the Chief came home so fast, the sled almost upset."

"What got into you, old fellow?" Jim asked the dog. "You didn't see a wolf, did you?"

Pat answered for the animal. "We didn't see anything, but after we started home, we heard a noise. It sounded like a gun."

"Probably some trapper hunting his supper," Thorne told her. "Now you run inside while I put things away." As he loosened the leather gear, Jim noticed that the dog seemed unusually restless, but his master had no more idea than Pat how close both the child and Silver Chief had been to death. Had the men touched the child, the animal would have defended his charge savagely; handicapped by harness and sledge, he would certainly have lost the fight.

A few minutes later the officer hurried into the cabin. "Young Lady," he said, "Soapy has just driven up to the Post. I'm going to put coffee on, then go over to help unload. Soon as we've finished I'll bring him back here for grub."

Outside the store the community crowded in excitement around the mail sledge. Every dog in the settlement was howling its welcome to the newly arrived team, and men got in each other's way as they carried the sacks inside. In such districts as this, postal deliveries, the chief link with the outside world, did not come so frequently as in towns. Even those lonely souls who knew from long experience that the sacks held no letters for them awaited Soapy Andrews' arrival with eagerness, for in winter most of MacDonald's supplies came by mail.

To the waiting child the business at the store seemed to take hours, but at last the two men stamped into the police cabin with Silver Chief beside them.

"Hello, Pat!" Soapy said in greeting, as he set a package on the table and began peeling off his furs. "My, but that coffee smells good, Jim! I'm hungry as a bear after a winter's hiding. Some storm I ran into yesterday—much worse back there than you seem to've had here. Thought I wasn't going to make Cameron today. Glad I did though—I'm always sure of good grub with you. Well, guess I'd better attend to business before I do anything else." He stopped talking and reached for the package.

Andrews was a big, heavy man with a body toughened by exposure to stormy weather. A thick beard almost covered his florid face and gave him a rather fierce expression. Only when he smiled could the good humor and kindliness be seen that won him friends wherever he went.

"This package," he began again with a twinkle in his eye, "is addressed to Miss Patricia Blaine. Anybody here know a young lady of that name?"

"That's me, Mr. Soapy," Pat answered shyly.

"Well, so it is, so it is!" he said, as if greatly surprised, and handed her the parcel.

The child turned it over in her hands wonderingly, and after a minute Thorne reached out and helped her untie the string. Wrapped carefully within a pasteboard box was a small doll with golden hair and blue eyes. At once, with a motherly gesture, Pat took it in her arms and began gently to stroke its hair. Before this time she had owned only a rag doll made by her mother, and had never even imagined one like this. Satisfied by her pleasure, Jim caught Andrews' glance and smiled his thanks. Toys of any sort were scarce in the Hudson's Bay country, and the postman must have done some real hunting to find this one. The little girl had not yet mentioned a letter, and before she could ask whether her father had sent the package, Thorne hurried to the stove and said, "Chuck will be ready in a few minutes, Soapy. If you want to wash up, now's the time to do it."

Not until Pat had taken her new treasure to bed and Andrews was also asleep, did Jim find time to give serious consideration to his own affairs. On receiving his letters at the store he had read them hastily. Those from home would go with him on the trail tomorrow. The communication that troubled him was another cryptic message from the Chief Inspector: "Important to consider everybody under suspicion."

What under the sun had got into the Old Man lately? Consider everybody under suspicion of *what?* This was certainly one blind job. Everybody might mean Bill or Danny or Doc Wallace on routine health inspection of the district. His eyelids suddenly flew wide open. It might even mean kind old Soapy sound asleep across the room.

At this rate, if I run into trouble I won't dare to count on anyone, Thorne said to himself. Well, that had happened plenty of times before. A Mounty was trained to work alone, and in emergencies Silver Chief was equal to another man. Policemen always had to suspect the innocent until the guilty had been caught, but he didn't like having to keep a watchful eye on old friends. The next minute he punched his pillow and turned over. All he needed was a good night's rest, and he was going to get it.

V

"MEBBE SIX, MEBBE SEVEN"

LONG before daylight Thorne sat down to breakfast with Pat and Soapy Andrews. The child was still too delighted with her doll to eat much. Even the fact that Sergeant Jim and the Chief were going away and that she was to stay at the store took second place in her thoughts.

"Too bad you're not hanging around another hour, Jim, until I get things loaded up at the Post," Andrews said as he finished. "We could go part way together on the Aklavik trail."

Instantly the officer's mind was on the alert. To keep from answering at once, he lifted his coffee cup to his lips and drank slowly. Why was Soapy so sure the patrol duty would be along the Aklavik trail? There was an equally good route northwest into the bush, and Jim had not yet mentioned to anyone which one he planned to follow. Was it because the postman had broken the way from Aklavik coming in yesterday afternoon, and therefore supposed any driver would prefer that to the other? Perhaps he had some reason for wanting a member of the Mounted Police to stay off the northwest road, or had he made the remark hoping Thorne would hurry ahead on the Aklavik trail and be out of the way?

These suspicions probably had no foundation, Jim told himself, but he made up his mind to hang around the extra hour and see for himself what was loaded on the postal sledge. To use the Aklavik trail part way was no great inconvenience. If he did not want to stick to it, there were several places where he could turn off the road and cut across country to the other route.

"You know," he said, finally, setting down the empty cup, "I think I'll take you up on that and tag along."

"Fine! Fine!" was the reply. "I'll go over now
and look after the team. By the time I get that
done, Mac will be ready with his stuff."

From long practice, Thorne moved swiftly
about the remaining chores. His sledge had been
loaded before breakfast. He cleared away the
dishes and killed the fire. After harnessing the
dogs, he bundled Pat and her few belongings on
top of the load, swung the heavy door to, and
pushed the hasp peg down firmly through its
staple.

When they drove up to the Post, Soapy, Danny,
and Mac were just beginning to haul out mail
sacks. All the villagers who had no pressing business elsewhere drifted gradually up to the sledges.
This double departure of postman and policeman would be the high moment of Cameron's
day.

Little Pat, cuddling her new doll, attracted
much interest, for she looked very different from
the other children in the settlement. Watching,
Thorne said to MacDonald, "Looks like you're going to be popular these next few days."

Mac smiled dryly. "I s'pose so. Danny's been
fussin' around all mornin' like a hen with a new
brood of chicks. You're takin' an awful chance
leavin' the youngster with two old child-spoilin'

bachelors. . . . By the way, Jim," he added, "when do you expect to be back?"

"Can't say, Mac," Thorne replied cautiously. "Depends a good deal on the weather, of course. You know how it is."

Whether he did or not, MacDonald had to be satisfied with this answer. Either Jim Thorne's changed, the trader thought to himself, or his present job is even queerer than I thought.

Half an hour later the two teams surged forward, accompanied by a clamor of good-bys, whip-cracking, and howls from the dogs left behind. Soapy's sledge was first in line, and Jim gestured him to keep the lead; otherwise the Sergeant would soon have left his companion far in the rear. Andrews had a heavier load, and while his team was one of the best to be found, no lead dog in the district could equal Silver Chief in speed.

For the next five or six hours they drove over the frozen white crust. In all that time the postman made only one stop. In the North, loneliness forced men to gather together in small communities, such as Cameron, whenever possible. Single cabins were usually occupied by Indians or trappers out for a winter's work, and such people received little mail.

Jim's only job for the time being was to hold in his team. He kept a tight rein and let his mind dwell on the task before him. There had been nothing suspicious about Soapy's actions at the store, nor about any of the other men's, so far as he could tell. The mail sacks seemed to hold just regular stuff, and for personal use Andrews had bought only a tin of tobacco, explaining that his supply was running low.

Thorne was just about ready to write Soapy off the list of possible suspects, when the other's team abruptly came to a stop.

"What's the matter?" Jim called out.

"This gear is pullin' on the middle dogs and I might as well fix the lines right now."

"Need any help?"

"No, thanks. You go on, Jim. See you next trip."

With a wave of the hand, Thorne swerved his team and passed the other. Several miles farther on there was an Indian cabin. He planned to look over every place on the way, and stopping there would also give him the chance to see whether Soapy used more time than necessary for adjusting gear.

Dogs announced his arrival, and as soon as he knocked, a squaw opened the door a crack. At once her beady eyes noted below the parka the blue trousers with yellow stripes that were part of the Mounted Police uniform. Alarmed, she called a few guttural sounds over her shoulder to someone else, and a stocky man took her place at the door.

"What white policeman want?" he asked gruffly.

"Hot water to make tea," Thorne told him.

"Water not hot."

"I'll wait for it."

Grudgingly the door was swung more widely, and the officer entered the dirty, crowded room. Several children, an old grandmother, and a litter of Husky pups all watched his approach with apprehension. Jim sat down on a crude bench, lit a cigarette, and held out three to his host.

Many Indian cabins were filthy, but this was worse than most. The air was sickening from the odor of drying skins, greasy bodies, and food in a pot that the squaw was now busily stirring. She had already put on water in an iron kettle, and Thorne made up his mind to see that the stuff boiled hard before he used it. The window slits were glazed from years of smoke, but he had no need to look out—his team would let him hear when Andrews drove by.

"What's your name?" he suddenly asked the Indian.

"Tom Eagle's Nest."

"Been here long?"

"Four great snows."

Thorne slowly exhaled smoke. He was lucky to find an Indian who spoke this much English. His own knowledge of their lingo was limited to common expressions in half a dozen dialects.

He eyed the pile of skins and asked, "Just come in from your line?"

The other nodded.

"How many men back in there?"

Tom Eagle's Nest hesitated before answering. "Mebbe six, mebbe seven."

Thorne's interest sharpened. Since this Indian had been here four years, he knew well enough exactly how many trappers were working his district—there was no guessing about it. How to persuade the fellow to tell more was the problem. The cigarettes had made him talk this much, but if he thought the officer was trying to pump him, he would shut up like a sprung bear trap.

Jim finished his smoke, forced a yawn, and stared at the kettle. A thin steam was rising from it. In another minute or so there would be no excuse for staying longer in this shack.

"Anybody sick around here? Doctor Wallace wants me to let him know."

Tom Eagle's Nest shrugged his shoulders. "Nobody say."

"I'll ask at the other cabins. Who's out in the bush?"

The Indian named six trappers, two of his own people and four white men.

"That's six. You said maybe seven. Who's seven?" Thorne asked and yawned again to give the effect of being bored by this business of asking routine questions.

The impassive face never changed expression. "Tom not know. Mebbe man, mebbe spirit. See tracks, not moccasins, not snowshoes."

"Leather boots?"

"Mebbe."

"When?"

"Day before storm."

"Where?"

"Water boiling," the Indian replied, as if he had not heard the last question. "Policeman make tea here?"

"On sledge."

So that's the end of the conversation, is it? Jim said to himself, and reached for the hot water. As he did so, the dogs outside sounded their warn-

"Tom not know, mebbe man, mebbe spirit."

ing of an approaching team. That meant Soapy was on his way and in good time. To make sure, he stepped to the door and looked out. There was no mistaking the post sledge.

Fifteen minutes later Thorne turned his team and went back to the spot where he and Andrews had parted. There were no signs of other tracks. This was proof that the postman had met no one and that the halt had been, as he had claimed, merely to fix gear, and was not prearranged. For the time being, the officer could put doubts about one friend, at least, from his mind.

He now cut abruptly across country into the bush. This course would keep Tom Eagle's Nest in the dark for a few hours about Thorne's movements. Indian "grapevines" carried news fast. By tomorrow every redskin and half-breed in this neighborhood would know that a member of the Royal Mounted had come by, and on what trail he was traveling. Before that time, he hoped to surprise a few of them.

Warmed by tea and food, Jim rode the runners and let the Chief set his own pace for the team. On receipt of that last puzzling message from the Inspector, the officer had increased his food supplies for the trip. It was a good thing, too, for this patrol was going to take longer than he had first expected. Now that the storm had wiped out all tracks, his work would be much like hunting for a needle in a haystack, and particularly so when there was no description of the needle to guide him. He had learned one thing from Tom, though—this assignment had nothing to do with fur stealing, unless the theft had occurred on the Upper Cameron. Most Indians were given to few words, and usually they refused to discuss anything with a white man. It was different when lines were robbed. Then they expressed themselves fully and freely and lost no time before doing it.

Thinking over that conversation in the cabin, the Sergeant smiled dryly to himself. Tom Eagle's Nest might believe that a spirit wore leather boots for trekking up here in midwinter, but Jim Thorne certainly didn't agree with him. Such footgear meant a white man—a white man who was a stranger to the North. No old-timer would move five yards without snowshoes. For that matter, snow as deep as this would make walking without "webs" impossible for any distance. Who had tried to do the impossible was the first thing for him to find out.

VI

"PIERRE, YOU HAVE CRAZEE DREAM!"

THREE days later a baffled Sergeant pushed through growths of spruce along a stream. He would follow this last trapping line on his list until he met with its owner, Pierre le Brun, or, as everybody called him, French Pete. The small, wiry Frenchman was one of the few men around Cameron that Thorne had known before. Pete kept a clean cabin, and that meant a decent night's rest for the officer and his team. The trapper liked to talk, too, and if he had seen a stranger lately, he would not hesitate to say so.

In spite of these encouraging facts, Jim had very little hope of gaining any information. Since leaving Tom Eagle's Nest, he had used every means possible to learn something more about the boot tracks. The effort had been useless. If the trappers, white or Indian, knew anything, they were keeping the knowledge to themselves. Occasionally an Indian found great sport in fooling a white man, a policeman in particular. Perhaps the statements made by Tom Eagle's Nest had been for that purpose alone.

Darkness was falling when Thorne drove up to Pete's small winter shack. The Frenchman was out feeding his three team dogs. At their lines trappers kept the smallest team possible in order to save food supplies. Three Huskies were sufficient to carry a man back to Headquarters at the end of the season, or in case of illness. If his catch proved too great a load for the light team, he could go home, get extra dogs, and return to what had been left behind.

As the Chief, with the rest of Thorne's team, dropped flat before the cabin, Pete's Huskies made up in noise what they lacked in numbers. The Frenchman hurried to greet Thorne.

The Frenchman was out feeding his three team dogs.

"Come in, Sarzhan', come in! You are jus' in time to eat. Two days ago, I 'ear Sarzhan' on patrol. I say, 'Pierre, two, t'ree days, maybe he come by 'ere. Must have good souper dat night.' Today I roas' fresh deer meat an' feex big pot onion soup lak *ma mère* she make when I was boy."

"Sounds good to me, Pete," Thorne replied, already starting to unharness the team. "I'll be ready before you know it."

After the meal, Pete got out his mouth organ and played tunes that ranged from the old *voyageur* songs to more modern ones heard over MacDonald's wireless. When he paused to breathe deeply and wipe his mouth, the men talked about many things, including Silver Chief's last adventure.

"He one fine dog," the Frenchman said admiringly.

"You know Tom Eagle's Nest?" Jim asked abruptly.

Pete nodded.

"When I stopped in there the other day he told me some wild tale about finding boot tracks before the last storm. I think now he was just trying to see if I'd be interested in such news and go on a wild-goose chase."

Pete took the harmonica from between his lips and stared at Jim. "So—o!" he said slowly, "dat was no dream."

"What?"

"Day before storm, I come in from lines late. Down along reevaire bank, I see track. Dat not strange, no—mos' trappers cross ice down dere. Den I look some more; between tracks funny breaks in snow crust. I say, 'Pierre, dose funny. Look lak somebody wear boots. What fool wear dem in deep snow?' Dat night storm begin. Nex' day she too bad to go out. I feed dogs, go back to bed. Dream I fly long trip in airplane, go beeg town, sells skins for much monee. I wake up an' laugh at dream. After while, I remember track. I say, 'Pierre le Brun, where you get dose track? Same place you get dat airplane an' all dat monee. *Certainement*, you have crazee dream!' Maybe not crazee, *n'est-ce pas?*"

Thorne had been drinking in every word the Frenchman said. So Tom Eagle's Nest had not been trying to fool a policeman after all.

"Where did the tracks lead, Pete?"

Pete shrugged his shoulders expressively. "Back in bush, Sarzhan'. I no see ver' far."

"Think they had come across ice, do you?"

"Perhaps! Mebbe jus' follow reevaire bank. You look for somebody, Sarzhan'?"

Jim laughed, to throw the other off the scent. "If some white man's fool enough to trek in boots up here in January, I may have to take care of a frozen corpse. Explaining that will be much easier if I know where he came from. How about playin' that last tune again?"

Pete wiped his lips with the back of his hand and lifted the harmonica. Thorne listened with only part of his mind. Some tenderfoot stranger had come to the Cameron district in midwinter without necessary equipment. Was he alone or had he companions? And what was his business?

Next morning Thorne left Pete's early. He had intended returning to Cameron straightway. Instead he started out on a wider circle of the section just patrolled. With great care, his own supplies could be stretched to last another three days. If the dogs' meat ran low, a few hours of hunting would take care of that.

Exactly one week after driving off with Soapy Andrews, the Mounty returned to Cameron. The extra patrolling had yielded no results of any sort, and he had gone over every inch of the section with the utmost care. Of all the people he had met, only two men—one Indian and one

French-Canadian—had seen or thought they had seen a newcomer's tracks in the snow. Even these two agreed with all the others that they had seen no one who might have made the tracks. As far as Thorne could learn, the only stranger in the district that winter was a fifteen-year-old girl from outside who had come to stay with her sick sister, a trapper's wife. She was hardly the one for whom the Royal Canadian Mounted Police were searching.

Small Pat Blaine greeted both Jim and Silver Chief affectionately on their return to the Post. Mac and Danny seemed unwilling to let their young guest leave.

While the child was getting her things together, MacDonald said, "You can go out and stay just as long as you want to, Jim. Danny makes the best old-maid aunt you ever saw."

Hughes screwed up his face. "Mebbe so, but, Sergeant, it's Mr. MacDonald here that sits up nights worryin' what to write for next. Games an' colored hair ribbons an' candy an' blamed if I remember what all. Better build a lean-to on the police cabin to take care of the young 'un's loot when the next mail brings it."

Bill MacDonald's eyes twinkled as he struck

a light to his pipe. "Well, at least I didn't get up two or three times a night to see if she was covered warm enough."

As usual Jim Thorne laughed at the two of them. Back in the cabin he found that Pat already had some of the loot of which Danny had spoken. The trader had given her a small sewing kit with scraps of material from bolts of calico and gingham to make the new doll more clothes. Men like these who had no womenfolk to look after them soon learned to patch holes and sew on buttons. But these doll dresses made by Pat, under supervision from Mac and Dan, were certainly wonderful to behold. Jim found it hard to control his laughter when Pat showed them to him, though he had to admit he couldn't have done any better. At the first opportunity he would suggest that they hang the sign, "Dressmaker," on the Trading-Post door. Pat herself was completely satisfied with the results, and she spent most of her time dressing and undressing the doll.

It was plain that the toys and the visit to the store had both been good for the child. She laughed much more often and hummed little tunes to herself while playing about the cabin. Watching her, Thorne could not help wondering what sort of life she would have when her father took her up to the lonely mining claim.

The weeks passed. During that time the Mounty set out on frequent patrols and became increasingly familiar with the country around Cameron. No matter where he went, everything seemed quiet and peaceful. He had never known any district to have as little excitement. For once the officer wished that trouble might break out somewhere in the section and perhaps give him a real clue to what was doing.

This game of "Blind Man's Buff" was getting his wind up. It was now past the middle of February, and in all this time he had learned only one small item that might be used in a report to Headquarters: Early in January, on a day preceding a blizzard, two men had seen tracks that looked as if they were made by someone from outside wearing leather boots, instead of moccasins or snowshoes. No, they had not seen the wearer. For almost two months Sergeant Thorne had been running around in circles wasting supplies and time looking for this stranger or for anything else unusual that might be found. Had the men really seen the tracks? Well, that was what they had said. One was an Indian who thought a spirit might have done it; the other was a French trapper with plenty of imagination. Thorne squirmed as he pictured the men in the Aklavik office reading this report. For the first time in his life he was on the verge of going personally to Headquarters to admit that he could make no headway with an assignment.

Then unexpectedly one morning Pierre le Brun drove in from his lines to Cameron.

VII

A SMALL BLACK BOOK

AT THE Trading Post French Pete's business was to buy a new trap. The spring on an old one was worn out. He had been trying thriftily to make it last the season, but all of his attempts to repair it had been useless. In the past week two different foxes had managed to free themselves when caught, and their skins if perfect would more than have paid for a new trap.

Pete had not been in to the settlement since Christmas, and he had two months' catch to turn over to the trader for credit. When the skins had all been valued and recorded in MacDonald's book, the little Frenchman made his purchase and added to it a few staple groceries. Then for an hour or so he sat beside the wireless and listened to a program of music, and later the news. This was not encouraging. France lay crushed beneath the German conqueror's heel, and her chances of regaining freedom seemed far in the future. Pete was a veteran of the first World War. He was past the age for serving in this one, but he worried about the conflict much more than most of his neighbors.

Another customer or two now entered the store. After a few minutes of talk, Pete picked up his package and went out. Instead of directing his team back toward the bush, he went straight to the police cabin. The thought of making this call on Thorne had lent excitement to the trapper's life for several days. Stepping up on the porch he knocked firmly on the door.

Thorne swung it open and seeing who his visitor was welcomed him cordially. "What are you doing down here today, Pete?" he inquired.

The little man explained about the trap. For a while they discussed things of general interest, including the war news that had just come

over the air. Pat and Silver Chief were out playing, so the two men were alone. Finally Pete got
down to business.

"Sarzhan'," he began, "wen you left mon
cabeen, I no forget dose track. I walk down de
place on reevaire bank, but all lak new; no track
any kin'. I geev up. Yes'day, I go ovair lines, I see
fox geet away from old trap. He put up fight,
dat fellow. All aroun' snow ees mess up. Me, I am
ver' mad wid dat trap—dees second catch, it lose
me. When I pick up to take to cabeen, I see small
dark spot in snow." He reached inside his shirt,
pulled something out, and passed it to Thorne.
"Dees, Sarzhan'," he finished dramatically.

Jim looked at the object in his hand. It was a
slim, black, cloth-bound book about two and one-
half inches by four in size. He opened it curiously
and found that the first two thirds of the lined
white pages were neatly covered with script,
German script. He could not read a word of it,
but from the way the pages were spaced and
headed he felt certain it was a diary. And what
was a German's diary doing in Cameron district,
where to his personal knowledge there had been
no German for years?

Pete also recognized it for what it was, and
was asking himself the same question, Thorne

knew as he caught the trapper's glance. "It belong to one of the *Boche*, Sarzhan', *n'est-ce pas?*"

Jim nodded, then without much hope he asked, "Can you read any of it?"

"Me? non! I nevaire student, Sarzhan'. Francais, yes—a few words Anglais—no more."

"How did you know this was German?"

"I was born in Alsace—when I was small fellow see German every place, in shops, on walls," he answered simply, then as if the memory were hateful, he muttered a word under his breath.

Thorne knew a deep satisfaction. This little book might lead to anything. For the first time he felt absolutely certain that Tom Eagle's Nest and Pete had seen the tracks of which they had spoken. Tomorrow morning he would start for Aklavik with his find and have the Old Man put the office translator to work.

Only one thing troubled him now—Pete, as well as he, knew it was German. Well, there was nothing to do but trust the trapper to keep the secret. This he proceeded to explain.

The little man listened and seemed to take on a new dignity. "Nevaire fear, Sarzhan'," he said. "When I fin' book I say, 'Pierre, you no can fight dees war—perhaps de good God, he fin' dees way to let you 'elp.'"

Thorne stretched out his hand to grip the other's, then in a lighter voice said, "You must stay and have grub with us. I can't make onion soup like you, but I can stir up eggs with the best of them."

At that moment Pat came in with the Chief and was introduced. While Jim˙ cooked, Pete played his harmonica, and the child listened with delight. Soon after they had eaten, the guest left, and the Mounty began at once to prepare for the run to Aklavik.

Two days later he walked into the Chief Inspector's office and told his story. The Chief Inspector listened intently until the account ended. Then, turning the book over in his hand, he said, "Jim, if this is what I hope it is, even Ottawa will be interested. Now to find out!"

He pushed a button and within a few minutes the official translator was at work on the book, giving a running account of what was read. After the first page or two the Chief Inspector suddenly thumped the desk with his fist and exclaimed, "That's it, Jim, that's it!"

Thorne was still in the dark as to what the other meant. The diary had been started in an Internment Camp for Nazi prisoners, and the first third of the contents was what any home-

The Mounty began to prepare for the run.

sick captive in a strange land might have written. Then abruptly the subject changed to one more important: the possibility of escape.

From that moment, the two listeners never took their eyes from the translator until he had finished. When he left them, taking the book with him to make a complete written translation, the Chief Inspector turned to Thorne.

"Jim," he began, "that's the story the Government's waiting to hear. Last year when those other Nazis broke out of camp, it didn't take very long to recapture them. This time it was different. These two disappeared without a trace. One day they were there and the next they weren't. Nobody seemed to know when they got away from the camp—nobody saw them afterwards as far as Intelligence could discover.

"It was just as if the earth had opened up and swallowed them. The higher-ups made the decision to keep just as quiet as the Nazis. They let no word of the escape leak out, not even in the camp. There they just bluffed the other prisoners into thinking those fellows had been taken away for special questioning. Outsiders never knew a thing. Since the job had been managed so smoothly, there was no telling who had been working with them. And that was what had to be learned.

"When they called in the Force to help, they demanded that no orders go out, even in code, by wire or post. I, for one, objected. I said my men weren't used to working in the dark. I might have saved my breath. Those communications you got from me were dictated." Here he paused to chuckle. "I could just imagine what you thought when you received them. It wouldn't have surprised me to see you walk in any day."

Thorne grinned. "I came pretty close to it, at that."

After a minute the other resumed, "Well, now we know from that diary the two worked alone, sharing plans with no other prisoners. On the outside, the fact that they could both speak English well was what helped most." He paused again. "Funny they should have come our way and landed in the Cameron district. They're being hunted in every part of Canada."

"Where do you suppose they're bound for?" Thorne asked suddenly, adding, "certainly not much farther north, where they'd land in the Arctic Circle."

The Old Man's eyes narrowed. "Well, the diary shows that they have this Northwest Territory correctly mapped out in their minds, even if they didn't put down where they planned to go. That's where they were smart. I'm surprised they wrote as much as they did. Maybe they thought no one in Canada could read German script. As I see it, one of the greatest weaknesses of the Nazis is thinking everybody else is stupid." He paused to point to the large map of the territory above his desk. "As for going farther north, Jim, you've got to remember that while they know what a map says, they have no real idea what to expect in weather. You and I do. We think no man in his right mind would try to travel up here in winter without perfect equipment and supplies. These fellows didn't even have snowshoes. That's proof enough. Of course, by this time they may be sick of snow and ice and already headed southwest."

"You mean toward the Pacific Coast? Even if they ever arrived there what good would it do them?"

"Not much, I hope. But they may have some wild plan of meeting up with some of their allies, the Japanese."

"Where?" Thorne asked.

"Probably across the United States border. There are a good many Jap farmers in the Pacific Coast states, and since Germany and Japan are Axis partners, they doubtless have spies in those Japanese settlements."

"But how would they ever get across the border, when both we and the United States are watching every foot of land?" Jim wanted to know.

The other grunted. "I didn't say they would succeed, but they may make an attempt."

Sudden amusement flickered over the Chief Inspector's face. "All you have to do, Jim, is find them, and since they have only a few weeks' start on you, that ought to be easy."

"No job at all," Thorne retorted. "At least I know now what I'm looking for, even if they're too far ahead to see. May I have those descriptive forms again, sir?"

The next minute he was memorizing the information on these.

"Both educated, both blond, both in late twenties, speak English fluently. One five feet ten, stocky in build, blue eyes, right arm weak from wound. One five feet eight, slender, gray eyes, has first joint missing from small finger on left hand." He gave the paper back to the Inspector and watched him lock it away in the safe. Then after further talk, he rose to his feet. "I think, if it's all right with you, I'll get going. With weeks lost, we certainly can't afford to waste any more time."

The Old Man nodded. "I'll see that both the North and the West are on the lookout. Central and Eastern sections can call off the chase." He stood up and held out his hand. "Good luck to you, Jim! I'll be anxious to hear from you, but be careful how you word it. By the way, do you think that trapper can be trusted to keep quiet?"

"I think so, and, of course, he doesn't know the real story."

An hour later, having eaten and attended to several small errands, Thorne headed his team in the direction of Cameron.

VIII

THE LISTENER

DURING most of the journey back to Cameron, Thorne rode the runners and kept the dogs at top speed. The fugitives already had several weeks' head start on him and no more time must be lost in hunting them down. At last the job offered a satisfying challenge to his ability, and while he drove, he planned.

Silver Chief seemed to sense this change in his master and permitted no nonsense from the eight dogs he led. Like a small dark stream finding an outlet through imprisoning ice, the sledge flowed over the silent, blue-white fields. Occasionally it disappeared in wooded strips of fir and spruce trees, flushing small game by its swift approach. Under ordinary circumstances, Jim would have stopped to take a shot at these for the purpose of adding fresh meat to his stock, but today time was much more important than extra food.

In Aklavik he had purchased enough supplies to last for a long trip. Some of these could have been bought at Cameron, but the Mounty had decided against doing anything that might give away his game. If the two Germans were still alive, then somebody had certainly helped them; otherwise they would surely have perished in the vast expanse of snow and ice. He did not yet know who this helper was, and until he did, everyone in the district would have to remain under suspicion. It was absurd to think that Mac or Danny was a traitor to Canada. However, under the circumstances, he could not afford to trust anyone yet. When he closed the police cabin they would think that, for the present, his work around Cameron was finished.

In his own mind Thorne believed that the local accomplice was either an Indian or a half-breed.

Many of these people did not understand what the war was about and would have no hesitation about helping the enemy. He hoped this assistant, whoever he might be, was still with the Germans. If they had separated, the chase would be doubled, unless the Nazis, when captured, could be forced to talk. Most German prisoners, though, had a reputation for being sullenly silent under questioning. Perhaps Pierre le Brun could find a clue to the identity of the local helper. The little Frenchman had been in this district for a long time and knew nearly everyone intimately.

Any way you looked at this job it was going to be a lively tussle between wits, Thorne thought to himself. The Chief Inspector had told him to expect a stiff physical struggle as well, and if necessary, to shoot to kill. All that the Government demanded was the capture of the two men. Naturally, it preferred having them alive. If this were not possible their death would make no great difference. The small black diary had revealed all that was necessary about the escape.

As a result of the Old Man's warning, Jim had purchased extra cartridges, but he hoped these would not have to be used. The Sergeant, as did all his fellow-members of the Force, knew that his business was to track down offenders and turn them safely over, alive, to the proper authorities. Punishment was not his worry; that could be decided by regular processes of the law. In this case he hoped to follow his usual course —shooting to kill only in necessary self-defense.

The two Nazis, at large, were a menace to Canada and must therefore be placed where they could do no harm. Aside from their evil part in this war, he had a feeling of understanding for them. Had he been imprisoned in Germany, as they had been in Canada, he too would doubtless have tried to escape. Later, he was to look back on this moment and wonder why he had ever felt even this fleeting kindness toward them.

The problem that really troubled him on this drive concerned small Pat Blaine. If the Germans were in hiding somewhere, waiting for spring to make the trekking easier, this job might take two months. Mac and Danny were fond enough of her to keep her that long at the Post, but Jim, having promised to let her father know of any change in affairs, determined to do so. Frank Blaine was the one to take full responsibility, even though the child might want to stay in Cameron. At the lonely mining claim she would miss the affectionate companionship of the men and of Silver Chief. So far Blaine had not written his daughter a line, and when she reached home, he was not likely to spend either thought or money on making her happy.

In a recent letter, Frances, Jim's wife, had suggested asking Blaine to let Pat live with them, but the Mounty did not believe in such arrangements. You never knew where you stood. Some day Blaine might suddenly decide he wanted his daughter back. When that time came she would probably be more unhappy about going home than at her present age. Poor little tyke, Jim thought pitifully, and wished someone else had the job of breaking the news to her in Cameron.

On reaching the settlement around noon, he went straight to the police cabin. After releasing the dogs and eating a hurried lunch, he began carefully to reload the sledge for a long trip.

Meanwhile, Silver Chief had sought out Pat and together they came running home to Thorne.

"My, I'm glad you're back, Sergeant Jim," the child exclaimed. "I like to stay at the store but I'd rather be here with you and the Chief."

Thorne patted her on the shoulder and thought unhappily that this was probably as good a time as any to tell her the truth. "Young lady, I have some real news for you," he began. "I have to close the cabin today. That means your father will come soon and take you home with him."

The dark eyes widened. "But Sergeant Jim, my mother won't be there, and. . . ."

The officer forced lightness into his voice. "That's why you must be a big girl and help your father. He hasn't anybody except you now."

The little girl's lower lip was quivering but she did not cry. Thorne thought it might have been easier for both of them if she had.

In a low voice she asked, "Will you bring the Chief to see me some time?"

"I'll do that my first chance, Pat, and I'll write Donald to send you some pictures of Silver Chief. What about your own Huskies? Your father had five in his team down here, didn't he?"

"Yes, but they're old and cross. My father won't let me pet or play with them, like I do the Chief. Once I had a little puppy . . ." She stopped suddenly and Thorne made no comment.

The puppy had probably been sold, as was the custom where dogs were so valuable to men.

"When will my father come, Sergeant Jim?" was the child's next question.

"Maybe in a week or so. I'm going past your home soon and tell him you're waiting here at the store."

"May I take the doll and the things Uncle Mac got for me?"

Jim nodded. The next minute she brightened into a smile. "Uncle Danny made me a little bed for the doll. He painted it red and I fixed a cover from a torn piece of fur. I'll show them to you when you're at the store."

"Fine! Now you get your things together and carry them over to the Post. Then when your father comes they'll all be in one place, and you won't leave any behind."

After she went out the door the Mounty set to work in earnest. By two in the afternoon he was ready to leave. Stopping at the Post, he found several men from the village hugging the stove and listening to the radio. Thorne nodded a greeting to the group and strode over to Pat who was waiting to show him her latest possessions. When these had been duly admired, he walked to the fur room, where MacDonald was sorting skins.

"Did those just come in?" Jim asked.

Mac nodded. "It's been a good season so far," he said. "Even the laziest trappers have something to their credit. Pelts are thick and in fine condition, too." The trader now turned abruptly to face the policeman. "What's this Pat tells us about you leavin' and her goin' home?"

"That's what I dropped in to talk about, Mac. There just isn't enough excitement in Cameron to warrant having a policeman hang around longer. I promised Blaine if I had to go before April, I'd let him know so he could come for the youngster."

"Danny and I'd be glad to keep her till then."

"If you want me to tell Blaine that, I'll do so, though I believe every day she stays here is going to make it harder for her to go and for you to give her up. I know how I feel about the young- ster, myself."

"I s'pose you're right, but we'll certainly miss her. Having her around has made Danny ten years younger. He's goin' to have a fit when Blaine takes her."

"Where is Danny?"

"Choppin' wood. When Pat brought the news he went out without a word and hasn't come in again. By the way, how do you plan to send Blaine word?"

"I'll probably go over the district once more and take in his place on the way."

"That means she'll be around here a while yet. If I know Frank Blaine, he won't hurry too much. Leavin' that claim of his is the last thing he'll want to do—no matter what it's for. That sounds

mean but I see red whenever I think of the way
he's neglected Pat. If she was my little girl,
nothin' in the world—certainly not a two-by-
four wash of gold—could keep us apart." Mac
stuck his pipe in his mouth and clamped his teeth
on the stem.

It was not often that the trader became really
upset about anything, Jim knew. If this were a
sample of how the two old bachelors felt about
the child, he was getting out in a hurry. He had
no desire to have Danny, that old blunderbuss,
blow up in his face.

Putting an end to further conversation, he
said, "Well, Mac, it's been nice seeing you again
this winter. You'll be hearing from me."

"Good luck!" MacDonald called after him.

As the officer passed through the store, the
three other men followed him outside. Pat was
on her knees in the snow, petting the Chief where
he lay at the head of the waiting team. Danny
stood beside her, cautiously watching the other
eight dogs. Showing favoritism to one member
of a harnessed team was a dangerous thing to do.
Even these Huskies voiced an occasional growl,
but no one of them made a move. All had a whole-
some respect for the Chief's strength. In the past
each at some time had locked with him in battle.

Pat was on her knees in the snow, petting the Chief.

Having survived such an experience, none wished to repeat the performance. That this terror they feared and obeyed would now lie still while a child scratched his head was always hard for them to understand.

With the man all of them behaved, for he was master and had the power to punish. This he seldom did, though he made them work to the limit of endurance when on patrol. Had the animals been able to express themselves in words, they would have had only one complaint—the lead dog. The Huskies all sensed that Silver Chief was not really one of them. Yet, whatever that creature dictated was law for all the rest.

On the step, Thorne stood still for a moment and watched the little girl. Then he went forward, lifted her up and hugged her. "I'm going to tell your father you're the nicest daughter a man could have," he whispered, placing her again on her feet.

Hughes stood by in silence, looking as if the sky were about to cave in on him.

With a "So long, Danny! See that Mac behaves himself!" Jim boarded the sledge, cracked the whip, and was off.

"Sergeant Jim, please tell my father . . ." Pat called after him.

In the clamor of departure the Mounty did not hear, and the child let the message hang unfinished on the frosty air.

No one seemed interested in what she had started to say, except one of the men standing by. With narrowed eyes he stared at the ground. When the sledge had gone from sight, he re-entered the store with the others, collected his things, and left. Outside, he stood by the main trail for a moment of indecision and muttered to himself. Then he turned sharply and following a short cut through the spruces, disappeared from view.

IX

THE EMPTY CUPS

NOW on the chase in earnest, Thorne determinedly put from his mind the unpleasant memory of the recent parting with small Patricia Blaine. From this moment until the Germans were safe in his custody, every waking thought would be given to his job.

The first thing to check was whether Tom or Pete had seen the tracks later and in which direction these were pointing when seen. From both accounts the day had been that preceding the storm, and the French-Canadian had mentioned the time as near dusk. Unfortunately, he had also admitted paying little attention to them. This would not be true of Tom Eagle's Nest. An Indian's eyes photographed every minute detail, and so Tom must be persuaded to talk.

Arriving at the Indian's cabin, the officer called from the sledge. Moving like most of his race, with deliberation, Tom opened the door, peeped out, then approached.

After a brief greeting Jim began, "The trader told me you used to make the best bow sets in this district. I have a son about the age of your oldest. Would you make one for him?"

"Mebbe in summer. How big boy?"

Thorne measured with his arms.

"Policeman be in Cameron in summer?"

"If I'm not, give it to Mr. MacDonald at the store. He will pay you and mail it to me."

The Indian grunted his willingness to do this. Pulling off a glove, Jim fumbled inside his clothes and handed over several cigarettes. He replaced the glove slowly, playing for time to shape the question that must be made.

To his amazement Tom Eagle's Nest spoke first: "Policeman ever find strange white man's tracks?"

"Tracks?" Thorne asked vaguely, as if memory had failed him.

"Boot tracks in snow."

"Oh, those tracks that you thought belonged to spirit? No!"

The Indian's lips twitched in a small, superior smile. "Not spirit. Two suns later Indian see same thing where river bends below fir trees."

"You?"

"Little Wolf—my sister, his woman."

"Where were they going?"

"South."

"What makes you think they were a white man's?"

For a second Tom's narrow black eyes widened. "No Indian that big fool," he answered promptly.

"Well, whoever it was must have been drunk or crazy. If your people find body when thaw comes, tell the trader."

Tom was plainly amused by this suggestion. "Wolves not leave body, only clothes."

Thorne forced a smile at this bit of gruesome humor. "Don't forget that bow," he reminded Tom, then drove away.

What luck, he said to himself, that he had thought of the bow. The Indians nowadays preferred to use rifles in hunting, but every once in a while you found one who still took pride in making good bows and arrows. Tom Eagle's Nest was one. MacDonald had once mentioned this fact in Jim's hearing, and the memory had helped in the nick of time. His son, Donald, already had several such weapons, but this extra one would be money well spent. It had succeeded in loosing an Indian's tongue, with the result that Tom himself had asked the first question about tracks. His further remarks had given the Mounty more definite information than had been expected.

Two suns after the night of the storm, the Germans had gone south from the river bend below the firs. That spot was just about ten miles from here and four or five southwest of French Pete's winter cabin. There was no need to waste more time stopping between here and Pete's, and immediately Thorne headed the team that way.

LeBrun had almost finished his supper when Jim drove up, but in a short time he placed another good meal before Thorne. This evening there was no harmonica playing. As soon as dishes were cleared Jim got down to business.

"Pete," he said, "I'd like to find that German who lost the diary."

"He is bad man, Sarzhan'?"

Thorne evaded this question with a shrug of the shoulders. "He is a German, and this is wartime. I don't believe he can cause much trouble here in the bush, but if he manages to get outside, who can tell what might happen? Two days after you saw tracks there were more at the river bend below the firs. They were headed south."

"So-o! You want me help fin' dat fellow?"

"I want you to try to find out who was with him. Pete, the German was on foot and without snowshoes. If he's still alive, somebody around here helped him—that's certain. If we can locate the helper we can get the German, I believe."

The other man seemed lost in thought. "Firs' I fin' out who need money mos' dis winter, an' who spen' it."

Thorne nodded. "That's a good idea. Keep your eyes and ears open and your mouth closed. No one must guess you are interested. Anything you learn may help Canada, and France as well."

"You be in Cameron long, Sarzhan'?"

"No, I have some business elsewhere and I've closed the cabin."

"Where can I sen' word?"

Jim wrote his name on a slip of paper and addressed it in care of the Chief Inspector, at Aklavik.

Pushing this across the table, he advised, "Hide that carefully! No one must know that you are helping me. If you learn anything important, write: 'This season's catch is good!' Nothing more. If you need help urgently, write: 'Foxes are running!' In that case I, or someone else, will come down to take over."

Pete repeated the messages several times, then folded the scrap of paper with the address and hid it in a chink between the wall logs. The responsibility warmed his heart.

"I try ver' hard, Sarzhan'," he promised, "for Canada an'," he paused sadly, "for La belle France."

"I believe that, Pete," Thorne assured him. "Now I'm going to turn in, so I can get an early start in the morning."

A few hours later he was up and on his way southwest. In good time the sledge reached the small Indian village where Little Wolf, brother-in-law to Tom Eagle's Nest, lived. The Mounty had been here on a previous patrol, but had learned nothing that time. Yet Little Wolf had known then about the tracks. Jim wished he knew which one of the fellows who had come outside might be Little Wolf. To ask for him directly would give away Tom Eagle's Nest. That might cause not only a family feud, but all the Indians around would cease being friendly to the Royal Canadian Mounted. This was something Thorne did not want to happen.

As on the earlier occasion, he asked routine questions about health and the season's catch. Without much hope he repeated, "Any new people come up here?"

They answered "No," and that was all.

Jim soon drove off. About a mile or so down the trail, a shadowy figure slipped from behind a spruce tree and hailed him. The officer pulled on the rein. The man was a young brave perhaps twenty years old, who had been at the village. He began to speak swiftly in his own tongue, and Thorne was soon at a loss.

"English, English!" he ordered and the other haltingly obeyed.

Using phrases from both languages, the conversation was gradually pieced out. Two days after the big storm, a sledge with three white men had passed below the young Indian's trapping lines. One rode the runners; the other two seemed sick and took turns riding the sledge. The team was small and they traveled slowly. Hidden from them, he had watched for a few minutes, then followed them for a little way.

Jim interrupted the account here by asking, "Why?"

The Indian confessed that he was curious to know why they did not stick to the trail. Instead they traveled by unbroken short cuts, as if afraid to be seen. When he turned back, they were going south. Two days later he saw the driver come back on the sledge alone.

Having listened to this much, Thorne broke in again, "Why tell me this?"

Because, the Indian went on, late yesterday that driver had been seen going very fast over the same short cuts to the south. The brave thought the policeman ought to know.

Jim listened with his tongue in his cheek. Strange Indians never gave away information without a purpose.

"Who were these white men?" he asked.

"Not know."

To himself Jim said: You know the local driver all right, and if you think you're fooling me, guess again. You've got some score to settle and you think if you put me on his trail, the law will take care of him for you. Aloud, he expressed thanks and promised to keep the matter secret. Before he could say any more, the Indian turned and slipped away into the bush.

Hidden, . . . he had watched for a few minutes.

What has suddenly got into the Indians around here? Jim asked himself. Two, within twenty-four hours, had given a Government officer clues. He smiled dryly. Maybe if I just go back to Cameron and sit down, they'll take over this job and finish it for me! Well, whatever that fellow's grudge may be, it's done the police a service. I'm sure the trail lies straight south for a while, at least. He caught up the whip, then paused. It might be a good idea to go back to Pete's and talk with him. There was a chance that the trapper would know if this fellow and some white man had been having trouble. The next minute he decided against this. To save time seemed more important than anything else right now.

"Mush, Chief, mush!" he said sharply. The next moment they were racing down the trail.

The rest of that day and the following one Thorne learned nothing further. The country he passed through was barren, with few cabins. The occupants of these insisted that they had seen no strangers in months. Around noon a light snow began to fall, and he urged the team forward to the destination he had in mind, Frank Blaine's place. There Jim hoped to spend the night, and also to learn if the Germans had come this way. Blaine might be a poor sort of father but there was no reason to doubt his loyalty to Canada. If the enemy had been here, the prospector would certainly tell a Government officer without being asked.

It was nearly three o'clock when he reached the spot where he expected to find Blaine. A broken trail still showing through the fresh snow led him finally to a cabin. When no one answered his call, Jim stepped off the sledge, then paused to watch the Chief. Sniffing and straining at his harness, the dog seemed greatly disturbed, and his master wondered if the animal's memory of Pat could possibly be mixed up with the scents around here.

Suddenly Thorne was struck by the deep silence of the place. No dogs were barking to announce the arrival of his own team. That was queer. He strode up to the building, knocked, then entered. The room in which the Mounty now found himself was cold and empty. Everything was in disorder, as if someone had left in a great hurry. Where would anybody so devoted to his place as Blaine go at this time of year? Could the man have possibly become homesick for his daughter and started for Cameron? That would account for the missing dogs. It would also be one piece of bad luck, Jim thought, now that he himself had troubled to come so far off his trail. Well, at least he could rebuild the fire, prepare food and sleep here, though he certainly didn't think much of Blaine's attempts at housekeeping.

The Chief was whining in his throat. Thorne stepped outside, released the lead dog, and put the others under shelter. Carrying snowshoes and supplies, he re-entered the cabin. Silver Chief pushed ahead, still growling ominously.

"What's the matter, Old Fellow?" Thorne asked, then turned again to his own affairs.

When the fire was crackling in the stove, he went over to the table, and like one suddenly hypnotized stood staring down at it. There before his unbelieving eyes were three emptied coffee cups, their dregs frozen to a muddy brown. Three cups, and Blaine lived alone! In that case who had used them? In the Canadian Northwest tea was a more popular drink than coffee. However, suppose that Blaine liked coffee—that accounted for only one cup. What about the other two? In midwinter nothing less than a great emergency would bring a visitor here, and the officer's suspicion fell at once on the two Nazis. If so, their local helper had left them before reaching Blaine's place. On the other hand, suppose that he, not Blaine, was the third coffee drinker. Then where was Blaine?

The Mounty glanced about the room, his eyes now taking in every detail. Bunks were stripped and the shelves almost empty of provisions. At the time of his arrival, both stove and room had been as cold as outside. That meant no one had been here for twenty-four hours at least. Even in the bitterest weather, an atmosphere of having been lived in clung that long to the interiors of these stout, well-chinked log buildings. This was probably due to the dry air resulting from a continuous roaring fire when a cabin was occupied. After a day, dampness and cold did their work thoroughly.

Well, standing here was getting him nowhere. Darkness was already shadowing everything. He must find their trail at once. By morning, if this snow continued, all tracks would be covered.

He turned to the dog, still prowling restlessly about the room. "I'd like to know what's got you so upset," Jim told him, as he put on snowshoes and caught up a flashlight. "Come on, let's see what we can find."

X

FRANK BLAINE WRITES A LETTER

SILVER CHIEF was troubled. Ever since he
had turned in the trail to this house, he had
been trying to remember something—something
that aroused a mixed feeling of fear and anger in
him. Inside the cabin he had almost known what
it was. Out in the air the thing was fainter, but
still present. When his master, after walking
about cabin and sheds, directed him again toward
the trail, the dog ran forward eagerly. Here, in
spite of falling snowflakes, he found the scent

strong until they reached the river bank. There he lost it and for a minute stood still, head stretched upward, sniffing. Then slowly he made his way out on the uneven ridge of ice. After going twenty or thirty feet he stopped. Here the clue had disappeared completely. Returning to the bank, he picked it up again, and as he ran southward, it became stronger.

In the course of a mile the scent was lost and found a dozen times, but the Chief pushed on, and as long as his master followed, the dog was free to pursue this instinctive urge. Once or twice Thorne was on the point of turning back, for he was uncertain about what the dog was chasing. Sensitive and intelligent though he was, even Silver Chief could not resist trailing wild animals when he was not on duty. His excitement today might be connected with something of this sort. What seemed unusual was that he had shown active interest while still harnessed as lead dog.

For Thorne all signs of a trail had ended at the river bank. Whether Blaine's sledge had gone north or south from there he could not tell. This snowfall, gentle as it was, acted as a blind. He could see only a foot or two ahead of him, and there was nothing to do but take a chance on the Chief's tracking, and follow.

It was now almost dark. Jim had about decided to return to the cabin when his dog swung abruptly to the left and climbed the low bank from ice-bound river to level ground. He focused his light on the place and found deep tracks that the afternoon's snow had only half filled. Here a heavily loaded sledge had probably pulled up the small slope, then proceeded inland. He looked about for a marker, for this was clearly the real starting point for his journey tomorrow morning.

Through the white, feathery air he finally selected a dead tree. This, slanting to one side, would serve the purpose very well. It had evidently been uprooted in some previous blizzard, but, clinging even in death to the soil, the trunk had not yet crashed.

With this decision made, Thorne turned around and roughed the dog's thick coat fondly. "Well, old fellow, you've done it again," he said, "but how you knew what I was after is beyond me. You might have linked Pat up with the cabin; you certainly couldn't have done that out here, and I don't know anything else to interest you. No, we're not going farther now. Come on, Chief, let's make for fire and grub."

As an extra precaution he paced the distance

back. Re-entering Blaine's cabin, he first added wood to the fire, then fed the dogs. After that he straightened the room, cleaned the dirty table, and started to prepare his own meal. In the north woods it was customary to help yourself to a meal wherever you found shelter. Since Blaine's shelves were so bare, Jim dug into his own supplies for everything except tea. There still seemed to be some of that in the prospector's tin container.

Pulling off the lid, the Mounty began to pour the dried leaves into the palm of his hand. A folded paper fell out with the leaves. Thorne dropped it on the table until he had brewed the drink. A tea can was certainly a queer place to stuff letters, he thought, starting to replace the sheet. Then, changing his mind, he unfolded the paper. The next minute the officer was completely absorbed in the effort to figure out the badly scrawled message the paper bore.

It read: "Anybody who finds this note—rush it to the Mounty at Cameron. He'll know what to do. The past three weeks two Germans have been hiding out here. Late one night I heard a sledge. It drove off before I opened the door. Two armed strangers pushed in. Have kept me prisoner ever since, making me take care of them.

Twice I tried to get away but didn't make it. The second time they knocked me out. Tonight, Tuesday, the sledge came again. It sounded like a small team. One German ran outside. The other covered me. After the strange team had gone the Germans told me to get ready for a trip early tomorrow. I don't know where. They have a map. I'll leave green wood on trail. If I can't get the best of them, and anything happens, I hope the Mounty will look out for Pat and see that she gets this claim. It's worth something. She's a good little girl. Tell her not to forget her mother. I meant to write but was too busy. Hurry. Frank Blaine."

The second time Jim read it more easily. In spite of the jumble of words put down in the dark, it was clear that Blaine had been given more schooling than most prospectors. The note had been written Tuesday night. That meant they had left Wednesday morning. It was now Thursday evening and they had thirty-six hours' lead. In his worried state, Blaine had written only the day instead of the date. If Silver Chief had not found the trail still fresh enough to pick up, Tuesday might have meant a week or two ago, instead of night before last.

Blaine had done two clever things, though. He

must have had very little hope that anyone would come along before spring. Yet he had risked writing the note, and had hidden it in the tea tin, the one thing any visitor was certain to open. Also, his plan to leave green wood on the trail would make anyone in the north woods know that something queer was going on, even if the note had not been read. No one would cut green wood at a camp site when plenty of dry was to be found.

Thirty-six hours, Jim repeated to himself. With fair luck he could overtake the other's team of five dogs (old dogs, at that) in a day or two. There was no time to lose, for he had an uncomfortable feeling about Blaine. The Germans were desperate men and Blaine would be no match for them in a fight, if it came to that. There was just one thing that might save the prospector. The fugitives must realize that a team driver familiar with the trail was necessary to their own safety.

So Blaine was not such a bad father after all. The last lines of the note showed a deep concern for Pat. Thinking over these things, Jim hastily ate supper and went to bed. The snow had already ceased falling and that was all to the good. In the morning he would be able to pick up their tracks much more easily.

At daylight, having reached the uprooted tree landmark, he slowed down the team. Unbroken except for evergreens, there stretched before him a clean crust of white that glistened even in the dim light of early morning. There was no good trail in this section, so he picked the least difficult through the bush, hoping the other sledge had traveled the same way. After two hours of such guesswork, he noticed a young sapling freshly broken. This might have happened from weight of snow, but the matter would bear looking into.

The next minute Jim was off the sledge examining the slender trunk. Ax marks showed plainly. Here they must have stopped to make a hot drink or to eat, and Blaine had made the most of the opportunity. There was no sign of the top where it might naturally have fallen. Then where was it? Looking around he finally saw the upper half. Only partly hidden by the fresh snowfall, it lay at a peculiar angle pointing southwest. There had been too little wind with the snow yesterday to carry the top branches to that position, so Blaine had somehow managed to throw it there.

"Well, Chief, southwest is the way we go," Thorne said, catching up the reins again and starting off. "Let's hope I'm not reading too much into these signs!"

Three hours later he found green wood again, and knew he was on the right track. This time the direction was straight south, the next time west, and just before nightfall south once more.

In the course of the day only four cabins had been passed. When he reached the fifth near dusk and found it empty, he decided to put up for the night. The fugitives must have had the same idea the day before, as the place had been recently occupied. This was proof enough that he was gradually catching up with them.

The next morning he saw the first sledge tracks. Several hours later the dogs began raising a fuss and came to a dead stop. Just ahead a dark object lay on the snow. Some frozen fox or wolf, Jim said to himself, and urged the team past. Then he drew in sharply, and halted a moment before going on, for the body was that of a dead Husky.

So they had lost their first dog. Now with only four to pull the overloaded sledge, the others were likely to drop fast. The Nazis had probably been forcing Blaine to drive at top speed. Even strong young animals could not have held up long under such conditions. Just as the Mounty expected,

The body was that of a dead Husky.

another dog was found that afternoon, and a third about eleven o'clock the next morning. It was pure luck that the wolves had not gotten to the bodies before he did.

From now on his job was simple. In an hour or so his team ought to catch up with them. The two dogs left of Blaine's five must be very weak. They would find it hard to pull the sledge and supplies. All three men were walking, for he could see tracks left by several sets of snowshoes. The Germans were no longer trying to trek with ordinary footwear in midwinter snows. Their accomplice must have equipped them properly, even though the tracks showed how little they knew about using webs.

A short way off to the left was a cabin, apparently empty, for no smoke curled from the chimney. He would stop there and get some hot food in him, before he raced onwards. Also, if everything went well, this might be a good place to put up for the night on the way back.

About noon Jim was on his way again. Refreshed by this unexpected rest, and spurred on by the Chief's tireless plodding, the dogs sped along the fresh trail. When they stopped the next time, they did it so abruptly that Thorne, absorbed in planning, almost lost his balance.

"Whoa!" he shouted, then noticed that the Chief was bending over something to the right of the tracks. At once the dogs behind him broke into a chorus of howls.

The next instant Thorne was beside the Chief and down on his knees in the snow. Lying on his face with arms stretched forward and a bullet in his head was the dead body of Frank Blaine.

XI

TANGLED CLUES AT CAMERON

THAT same morning, a number of miles northeast of where Thorne had found Frank Blaine's body, Pierre le Brun worked his lines along the Cameron in a discouraged mood.

His feelings had nothing to do with the catch. This was one of the best fur years that he had ever known. At the Trading Post, Mr. MacDonald already had a nice fat sum of Pete's credit and before the season ended that amount ought to be greatly increased. No other personal troubles weighed on the trapper's mind. He was in good health and had no responsibilities save for himself. Always he had been thrifty, like most people with French peasant blood in their veins, and the chief part of his earnings went out regularly by Postman Andrews to the Bank of Canada. This nest egg would take care of Pete in old age.

He was now fifty years old. He planned to stop trapping, after another winter or two and settle in the nearest small city. There, living carefully on his savings, he would enjoy plenty of music, people, and brightly lighted streets for the rest of his life. These were the things he had longed for during the years of hard work in the lonely, silent north. This morning he had no reason to think that anything would interfere with these plans, yet he was worried.

Suddenly he said under his breath, "Pierre, you were nevaire meant to be policeman. To trap wild animals, you are good, yes! To hunt men, no! Your brain, it is not beeg enough. For examp', dee Sarzhan', he look at man, he know dat man guilty. You, Pierre, you look at man many times, you still not know eef good or bad!"

After his last conversation with Thorne, French Pete had written down laboriously on a piece of brown wrapping paper the names of all the men he knew in the Cameron district. From these he would select those whom he thought might be willing to help a German. He still did not know that two men were involved, since Thorne had kept this detail secret. As good reasons occurred to him for scratching off names, he did so. When the list had been checked carefully several times, seven names remained. These belonged to three Indians, two half-breeds, a Swede, and another French-Canadian.

Pete's first suggestion to Thorne about seeing who had more money to spend than usual had gotten him nowhere. Everybody was profiting from this good season, just as he was. Even the poorest hunters and trappers now had something to their credit at the Trading Post. By midsummer when their winter's earnings would have all been spent, one could tell more about their needs. At present this information was not to be had.

The seven names left had been selected for varying reasons. The first five had all been in trouble with the law at some time in the past. To them "the country" meant the authorities who had caught and punished them for petty crimes. The question of patriotism would not bother them at all, even if they really understood what the war was about, which was unlikely. Any one of the five would snatch at a chance to make extra money, crookedly or not, if it could be done without too much risk.

The other two were very different cases. The Swede was honest and industrious, but he was known to favor the Germans. Though he talked very little, twice he had said stubbornly in a group at the store that he liked many Germans. In his native country they believed in being friendly with everybody. Pete was sure that the Swede was loyal to Canada, his adopted land, but his sympathies might tempt him to help a German lost in the snows.

The French-Canadian, Charlie, was lazy, shiftless, and tricky. More than one trapper in the past had felt that Charlie was to blame for a sprung trap, though no one had ever been able to pin the evidence of guilt on him. He would be just the sort to help the German—except for one fact: Charlie never lifted a finger if it could be avoided. He had been known to go hungry rather than work his lines or bring down his supper with a rifle shot. To picture Charlie struggling to rescue someone in a blizzard was beyond Pete's imagination.

Still, in spite of his doubts, he kept these seven

suspects in mind. When he met any one of the first five, instead of passing on with a brief greeting, he stopped and engaged the fellow in conversation. Pete was popular throughout the district. Even the Indians liked the tunes the trapper played on his harmonica, and as a result they talked more freely with him than with most white men. After several contacts with each of these, Le Brun reached the opinion that no one of them had dealt with a strange German.

This narrowed his suspicions down to the Swede and French Charlie. Aside from what he already knew about them, he learned an important fact: both needed money badly. The Swede's brother had been lost on a torpedoed merchant vessel and the widow had little means of support for herself and children except what her brother-in-law sent them from Canada.

For Charlie to need money was the usual thing, but now he planned to get married. This not only surprised Le Brun, it amused him. Since Charlie had never worked enough to support himself completely, it was to be hoped that the woman was strong and industrious, for she would certainly have to labor for both.

"Her name?" Pete had asked politely.

Charlie's little pig eyes had smiled slyly. He shook his head. At present that was a secret.

"So, Pierre le Brun," the trapper repeated this morning as he recalled his efforts to find the man Thorne wanted, "you were nevaire meant to be policeman. Here are two men—but which one ees guilty? You not know."

The occupants of the Trading Post at Cameron had no such problems. MacDonald and Hughes had forced themselves to accept the idea of losing the little girl, though Danny had found this very hard to do. The night after Thorne left the old fellow had fussed and fumed a good deal.

"I don't know why the Sergeant couldn't keep his mouth closed," he complained. "She could've stayed here all right until Blaine came in the spring."

"But Jim had promised if his plans changed to let her father know," Bill answered. "Jim was right about something else, too. He said the longer we kept her, the harder it would be to give her up. And that's the truth. You know it as well as I do. What's more, the youngster's beginning to like Cameron too well," he finished and pulled fiercely on his pipe.

Danny grumbled to himself. He wouldn't admit it in speech, but he knew Thorne and Mac were right. And if little Pat was getting to like it down here too much, that was bad. Yet it warmed his heart to think of it.

Even though he knew she had to go, he kept hoping she wouldn't. Every time he looked at the small figure playing happily with the toys he and Mac had supplied, the old man felt a fresh pang.

A week had passed since Jim's departure, and one night after Pat was asleep, Hughes asked MacDonald for perhaps the fiftieth time, "When do you suppose Blaine'll get here?"

"Danny, you know as much as I do," Bill replied patiently. "He may come tomorrow and he may not come until spring. If it's any comfort to you, I've had a hunch right along that we wouldn't see him soon. . . . What," he asked, abruptly changing the subject, "do you think Tom Eagle's Nest told me today?"

"What?" Hughes returned, stingy with words in his present unhappy mood.

"Jim ordered a bow set from Tom. I'm to pay for it and mail it on next summer when it's finished. What in the world do you s'pose made Thorne do that? He must have a dozen or two at home."

"Maybe he wants to give it to somebody."

"No, Tom said it was for the policeman's boy."

Danny could think of no explanation for this and remained silent. After a minute or so he suggested, "That's something Pat hasn't got. I wonder if she'd like one."

Mac hid his smile and answered seriously, "Better ask her. I don't know what she'd do with it, though. The way she pats all those dead skins the trappers bring in, I think she'd feel too sorry for an animal ever to aim at one."

"She wouldn't have to kill anything. I just thought I could put up a target and teach her to handle a small bow. Sometime it might come in handy."

"Maybe you're right at that," Bill told him. Later he thought, it's a good thing Blaine is coming. If the youngster stays around much longer, Danny'll never be able to give her up.

With her pretty, gentle ways, Pat managed to draw affection to herself. Almost everyone who came into the store paid her some attention, and even the roughest men seemed to understand that there must be no coarse talk when the little girl was present.

In Pat's eight-year-old head, the thought of leaving was now entirely in the future. Her days were filled to the brim with interest. There were times when she longed for her dead mother and at other moments she wished Sergeant Jim would come back and bring the Chief. Sometimes she wanted Silver Chief more than anything else. For long hours the doll, toys, and books would keep her busy. Then, like all children, she would long for some live companion, such as the dog, with which to romp. When she became restless, Danny would bundle her up and take her for a walk through the village; but willing as he was, he proved a poor substitute for a more active, younger playmate. Soon they would return to the Trading Post, and Pat would busy herself again with things inside.

At Thorne's suggestion, Mac had made the little girl responsible for some of the lighter household chores. Danny objected immediately, "I can do all the things needin' to be done around here."

For once, Bill lost patience. "Danny, you old idiot," he exclaimed, "what are you trying to do, spoil the kid completely? When her father takes her home, she'll be that much more unhappy if she can't help out some."

Hughes had said nothing more about this matter, knowing that he had been in the wrong. I'm just an old fool, he said to himself, and Mac's right.

A week passed and Blaine had still not come for his daughter. Perhaps it's just as Mac thought, Danny reminded himself happily, Blaine won't come for some time. He was considering this when a young Indian brought several pelts into the store one afternoon and asked for the trader. Directing him toward the rear, Hughes noticed that the fellow had been drinking too much, but Mac was used to handling such cases. Danny opened the stove and threw in another chunk of wood. There was the feel of fresh snow in the air. Also, his old bones had been aching all day, and that always meant falling weather.

A raised voice suddenly pulled him out of these thoughts. With MacDonald beside him, the young Indian was coming toward the door. His eyes were blazing. Danny heard him say something about white men being thieves. Then the door slammed behind him with a bang.

Pat who had been interested in a book at one side of the room looked up.

"How would you like to get your wraps on," Mac quietly called across to her, "and help Uncle Danny bring in kindling?"

She put aside the book at once and ran to get her things.

"What happened?" Hughes asked.

A young Indian brought several pelts into the store.

"Too much liquor, of course," Bill replied, "but something's behind that. He accused me of cheating him on furs, then went on to say that the white men always stole from Indians—if it wasn't furs, it was something else." Mac paused. "That young brave's always behaved himself till now. Wonder what's up? Too bad Jim didn't hang around a little longer. He might have found some of that excitement he was looking for."

Bundled up to meet the bitter cold just outside, Pat came forward. The next minute she and Danny had gone to get the wood.

Mac stood beside the stove lost in thought. He was glad no one else had been in the store at the moment, for trouble might have been started. Men's tempers were at their worst up here in midwinter. Loneliness added to several months of fighting merciless weather often turned a good-natured fellow into a bad one. There was a real grievance behind that young Indian's insults today. The trader had paid no attention to them; his one idea had been to persuade the youth to go home before Pat grew frightened or someone came in. The Indian had not only fussed about skins; he had also mentioned a girl. Well, one thing was certain: some white man had done the other an injury.

XII

SILVER CHIEF ENDS HIS SEARCH

IGNORANT of the mysteries developing around Cameron, Thorne knelt in the snow beside Blaine's dead body and wished that he had not stopped at the last cabin. If he had come along sooner the other man might have been saved. When a hurried examination showed that death had occurred several hours earlier, the officer felt relieved. It was interesting to discover that the Germans had wasted only one bullet on their victim. Did this mean that they were short of ammunition or so sure of their marksmanship that a second shot was considered unnecessary?

Blaine, poor fellow, had guessed that this very thing might happen. Three weeks of being prisoner to the Nazis in his own house, had given the prospector an idea of what to expect at their hands. In spite of this frightening knowledge he had risked writing his note and had slipped it into the tea tin under their very noses. Blaine had his faults but he was no coward, Jim said to himself. From the moment of the Germans' arrival, the prospector, taken by surprise, had been entirely at their mercy. Had he offered to co-operate, it was possible that they might have made a deal with him, as they must have done with their other local helper. Well, apparently he had not. Instead he had used his wits, the only weapon left him, in an effort to set the police on their trail.

Jim Thorne was as accustomed to the frozen gray northland and its cruelties as other men were to brighter, kindlier places. But today, looking at the dead prospector, alone and deserted in the snow, he was touched by sadness. The next minute his jaw set with grim purpose. Now he had to get the Nazis on two counts. They were not only enemy prisoners who had escaped from internment, but murderers responsible for the death of a Canadian citizen.

Making a swift decision, the Mounty placed Blaine on the sledge, urged the team around, and hurried back to the cabin so recently left. There the body would be under cover until he could return.

A little later the dogs were again racing down the trail. Permitted to set the pace, Silver Chief showed his team mates no mercy. Jim let his mind dwell for a few minutes on the Chief's actions lately. Something queer had been going on in the animal's mind ever since they had arrived at Blaine's cabin. The possibility that the dog had in some way linked up Pat with her home seemed the only explanation. Yet such a connection ought to include the child's father, and it had not. When Blaine's body had been found, Silver Chief was much less concerned than the other dogs with him. All the leader wished to do was to push on. His master was much too familiar with every move the Chief made not to understand what he was thinking. Furthermore, when ordered to turn back to the cabin, the dog had actually obeyed reluctantly. Used to perfect obedience, Thorne had been so astonished that he repeated the command sharply. To have his beloved mas-

ter use this tone with him made Silver Chief wince
as if he had been struck. His unhappy surge forward was so sudden he almost lifted his eight
team mates off their feet. He did not know why
he felt impelled to go in the other direction. Something kept pulling him that way, and because of
it his master was angry.

Jim was sorry he had been forced to speak that
way to anything he loved as much as the Chief.
On the other hand, if circumstances made it necessary, he would do the same thing again. Instant obedience was the first and most important
requirement of a lead dog. If he failed in this,
every Husky in the team would promptly do the
same thing. Then they would be no more good
to anybody.

Well, everything was all right now, for the
Chief was moving at top speed, and Jim began to
give full attention to what might lie ahead.

He was fairly sure that the Germans had only
two weak dogs left, and their progress must be
at a snail's pace, unless their local accomplice had
returned to aid them. The two men were ignorant of life in the north woods except for the
little they might have learned in these weeks as
fugitives. Since they were now having to break
trail for themselves, their map would be of no

use save to give general directions. The combined
dangers of wolves, freezing, and running out of
supplies faced them. They would hardly risk going too close to an occupied cabin—the next man
might not be as unprepared to meet them as
Frank Blaine had been. As for seeking refuge in
a settlement, if and when they finally reached
one, the Germans must have sense enough to
know that every Canadian was a potential enemy
of their race.

Also, what Thorne knew and the Nazis did not,
was that they would be suspected on other counts.
Strangers who traveled up here in midwinter
usually did so for no good purpose, and at the
first opportunity some citizen would report their
presence to the police. Too many criminals in the
past had tried to escape the law by hiding in the
Northwest Territory. Local inhabitants had
learned long ago that the best way to protect
themselves was to turn such matters over to the
Government.

All these things would work against the murderers. If, however, the helper had already met,
them on the trail, their circumstances would be
much improved. Also, his arrival could account
for Blaine's death. They would no longer have
needed the prospector, and for the sake of their

own safety they could not permit him to live. He knew too much.

Some distance back the officer had noted where the killing had taken place. From that spot to where the body had been found, bloodstains marked the way. Somehow, after being shot, the wounded man had managed to stagger for almost a mile over the trail homeward. Perhaps he had been trying to reach that last cabin, where Thorne had later carried him, for most men of the north dreaded the thought of dying in the open.

Even if the helper had met them; even if he had brought a larger team than might be expected from the statement in Blaine's note, Jim still had all the advantage, so far as overtaking them was concerned. No lead dog in the Territory could outstrip Silver Chief at his best, and the eight police Huskies were as good as could be found.

Every few minutes the Mounty drew rein and studied the trail. The men had floundered about so much that the crisscrossing of tracks made it impossible to tell how many were "mushing," or even if two sledges were traveling together. With startling suddenness the picture changed, for a second trail forked abruptly from the main one. The new tracks, evidently made by Blaine's two Huskies, climbed upward to the right through a forest of spruce. Continuing along the plain southward, a larger team of perhaps five dogs had cut its way.

As Thorne studied this puzzle, Silver Chief sniffed the air and looked anxiously toward the woods road, but he made no move to turn. Noticing, Jim said softly, "You may be right, Old Fellow, but I think we'd better follow the big sledge first. Now, hike, before they blow our heads off!"

With the team in motion again he felt safer. The fork had been in a dangerously exposed spot. Anyone hidden in the woods up the hill could have picked him off with ease. That would not be so simple while the sledge went at its present rate of speed.

Thorne was convinced that the fork was a trap. Ever since reading Blaine's note, he had felt that the fugitives knew the police were on their trail. Nothing else could so easily account for their hurried departure from the prospector's cabin. That was undoubtedly the news the local helper had brought them. How he had found out was the puzzle.

To two people only, MacDonald and Pat, had

Jim mentioned his intention to see Blaine. He had told Mac in the privacy of the fur room. Of course, it was possible someone in the store had overheard. He recalled seeing several men around the stove that afternoon. The trader had probably repeated it to Danny, but hardly to anyone else. Jim tried to recall just what he had said to the child. Well, whatever the words had been, the telling had been foolish. People were bound to talk to Pat about going away, and she would say naturally that Sergeant Jim had gone to see her father. At the time, he had not even dreamed of Frank Blaine's being mixed up with the Germans, but this was no excuse, he reminded himself. With everyone in the district under suspicion, he, an experienced policeman, should have realized that Blaine's lonely mining claim would make an excellent hideout.

While he thought, his eyes were on the trail ahead. Gradually a distant speck came into view, grew larger, and shaped itself into a dogsled. At last, he was no longer hunting shadows. Here was something real with which to deal.

The trail was still running parallel with the forest, and every once in a while he gave the slope a watchful glance. There was no telling where the sledge that had entered the woods might come out, or who would be with it when that happened.

As his own team crept up on the smaller one ahead, Jim became aware that it was being driven by an experienced man and that he was alone. This, then, was the helper. The two Nazis must have taken the woods trail.

Thorne was armed to meet any emergency. In a few more minutes he would overtake the accomplice, shoot over his head, and order him to halt. With that fellow safe in his custody, attention could then be concentrated on the woods.

Before he could put any of these plans into action, a shot from the forest whistled past him. Like a flash, the Mounty managed to turn his team and start back over the trail just covered. In a split second he had decided to sacrifice the local man for the Germans. They were his first job, and in that particular setup, they would have gotten him anyway before he could hope to get them. Their strategy was perfectly clear now. Doubtless they had heard his Huskies howling beside Blaine's body. Expecting Thorne to catch up with them shortly, they had first used the device of a forked trail, then, reaching a point where all the advantage was on their side, they had waited. The local man's sledge had served as bait. He had run no real risk. All that was needed was for him to keep just far enough ahead of the officer to avoid recognition. The Nazis would be ready to act the minute Jim's sledge slowed down. That was what they had done, but in spite of their marksmanship they had missed the first chance. They had also lost their helper, for in one glance backward Jim had seen the driver whipping his dogs frantically down the trail.

After almost a mile of back-tracking, he cut up the slope and entered the woods. There he settled the team in a secluded spot and released Silver Chief. Putting on snowshoes he started through the shadows with the dog.

The Chief was keyed up with excitement. Here he was able to follow instinct and work with his master at the same time. Left to himself, the dog would have rushed ahead, for each minute he was closer to solving his puzzle. Instead he was being held to a silent, cautious progress.

Thorne was certain that the Nazis, having seen him race back over the trail, expected him to do just what he was doing. Those two were far from stupid and were undoubtedly on their way through the forest to head him off. His chief advantage lay in familiarity with the north woods and in speed. As he slipped forward between the trees, he strained constantly to listen. After a time he paused abruptly. In the distance floundering steps could be heard.

At once Silver Chief growled low in his throat. Indian fashion, Jim hid himself in dense, low-hanging spruce boughs and whispered, "Down, Chief!" to the dog.

The animal dropped at his master's feet and Jim stood motionless, ready for any emergency. Voices could now be heard in snatches of whispering. Gradually one man, then a second, came into view. Although inexperienced in "mushing," they had sense enough to travel single file, separated always by several trees. In order to avoid being surprised, each held a pistol leveled directly ahead, yet it was clear they did not expect to run into him yet.

Peering through the boughs, Jim hastily identified them with the descriptions in the Aklavik office. He must remember that the taller, stockier fellow had a bad right arm. When they were about fifty feet away, he barked out the order to surrender.

Startled, both men fell back a little. Recovering, they fired at once in the direction from which his voice had come. The bullets embedded themselves in tree trunks.

"Down, Chief!"

Thorne repeated his command. Shots were again the response.

This time he let his own weapon speak for him, sending the first bullets over their heads, then aiming directly at the shorter man's wrist. The German's gun dropped; clasping his injured hand he turned and stumbled away through the trees.

In that minute of divided attention, the other German had crept up on Thorne's left. As he leveled his gun at the Mounty, a quiet gray shadow leaped from the ground and threw itself, full weight, against him. Together they went down in a struggling mass of desperate man and savage dog. There was a confusion of churning snow, cracking boughs, and an exploding revolver.

Torn by fear that the bullet might have hit Silver Chief, Jim rushed into the middle of this fight and separated them. Then, reassured that the animal was unharmed, he pointed to the other German, who could now be seen only dimly through the woods, and said, "Get him, Chief!"

At his feet the man who was supposed to be handicapped by a bad right arm lay with eyes closed, apparently exhausted from his struggle with the animal. His gun lay in limp fingers. As Thorne leaned over to grasp it, the fingers tightened like a flash and struck out with the blunt, heavy weapon. The Mounty received this unexpected blow on his shoulder. For a second he staggered back, then as the German attempted to rise, Jim knocked him down and, reaching for the right arm, gave it a twist.

The Nazi cried out with pain, and the next minute the officer had him disarmed and manacled. "Get up!" he ordered, then, "March!"

With a pistol against the prisoner's shoulders, he pushed him in the direction the Chief had just gone.

A few minutes later they overtook the second man. He was lying face down in the snow with the big dog standing above him on guard. When Thorne called off Silver Chief, the man continued prostrate, shaking with terror. It was plain that both of the Nazis feared this powerful animal more than bullets.

Jim bandaged the wounded German's wrist temporarily. Fastening his captives together and making them lead the way, he started in search of Blaine's missing sledge. As he had expected, the two dogs were already dead. Salvaging the few remaining supplies and blankets, he strapped them in bundles on the Nazis' backs.

In English as smooth as a professor's, the taller, stockier man now broke into dignified protest:

"You will pay dearly for this mistake, Policeman. Without reason you have arrested and injured innocent men. Now you would force us to carry for you like dogs. My brother and I are making a special survey of this territory for the Canadian Government. When the authorities learn how we have been treated, your career will be at an end."

For a second humor flickered through Jim's mind. They were undoubtedly making a survey of a sort, but it was a survey limited to routes by which they might escape from the country. They did not begin to guess how enormously interested the Canadian Government really was in the matter. As for threats to his career, Jim wished lawbreakers would find something more original to say. Almost every criminal he had ever caught had started out by giving him that warning.

This little byplay had not halted him one second in his work of securing their packs. As he finished, the shorter German added his bit. "You have not even told us why we were attacked and arrested," he said reproachfully. "Is this the justice the English talk of so much?"

"Since you're working for the Government you ought to know," Thorne replied easily.

"We do know," the other went on as if trying to persuade an unreasonable child to understand.

"And we know also that no fair-minded English officer would force a wounded man to carry a load. It is not sporting."

"But, you see, this is Canada," the Mounty returned. "Maybe we're a little tougher over here. If you'd been around a little longer you'd know Canadians think it isn't sporting to shoot an innocent man in the back. March!"

"You filthy swine!" the taller man blazed out suddenly.

"That's better!" Jim told him. "You sound more like a Nazi now. March, unless you want the dog to take care of you again!" Without another word they moved forward as he directed.

Having arrived where his own team was hidden, he rearranged the load and was soon on the trail northward. Jim's first thought was that they would have to seek shelter for the night in the cabin where Blaine's body rested. But he realized that at least two more hours of driving were possible before darkness shut down completely. He decided to push on and camp in the open.

The Germans marched along sullenly, stumbling as they went. Some of this was due to clumsiness with snowshoes, but a good deal, Thorne knew, was being done simply to delay progress. Each minute they could slow down the journey was an extra one in which to plan escape. It was also an extra minute of handicap for him.

He called out sharply, "Supplies are limited. The longer this trip takes, the less there will be to eat on the way. If you lose time for us, your rations will be cut in proportion. In that case you will grow weak and I may have to leave you on the trail."

The sudden manner in which their shoulders lifted told Jim that his words had given them hope. This was no moment for mercy.

At once he added slowly, "A starving man alone is no match for cold and wolves."

After that their pace was much steadier, and he had no occasion to speak to them again.

Once more in his place as lead dog, Silver Chief moved forward on the trail as fast as Thorne would permit him. For the first time in days nothing was pulling him away from routine duties. The tormenting scent of danger which his memory had somehow connected with these men and Pat still clung to them, but they were now safely in his master's keeping. When one of them had threatened Jim, the dog had found a savage delight in attack. Now he was satisfied; his personal interest in this chase had come to an end.

XIII

A RACE WITH TIME

THE frozen world was almost black with night by the time Thorne and his prisoners arrived at what he considered a suitable camping site. This, a small strip of wooded land, lay set apart from the snowy plain like an island in a river. It was not large enough to harbor wolves and there seemed to be, so far as could be seen through the dim light, a number of fallen trees to supply firewood in plenty.

Jim's first act was to tie the injured Nazi to

one of these dead trunks. Then, releasing Silver
Chief, he placed him as guard over the second
man and set this prisoner to gathering wood. As
the fire caught and flames roared upward, the
Mounty unharnessed and fed the team, then pre-
pared supper. When the silent meal had been
eaten, he took the ax from the sledge and helped
the wood-gatherer stack up enough logs to last
the night.

Only after these essential tasks had been done,
did Thorne get out his first-aid kit and attend to
injuries. The wrist wound was not a severe one;
swiftly it was cleansed and bandaged. Going to
the second man he used an antiseptic on the cuts
and scratches the German had received in his
tussle with Silver Chief. Jim's own shoulder
ached from the pistol blow. Examination showed
a large bruise, and for several days this would
continue stiff and sore. Under present conditions
this could not be relieved, so he paid no further
attention to it.

Efficiently the officer made arrangements for
the night. With the fire fed to last for hours and
his prisoners secured and well wrapped in all the
covers that could be spared from Blaine's supplies and his own, he set the Chief on guard at
their feet. With every weapon safe in his own

keeping, he crawled into his sleeping bag and promptly drowsed.

Years of such watches had made Thorne almost as alert as his dog. Each time one of the captives turned over, the Mounty's eyes opened. Once Silver Chief growled. His master awoke instantly to see one of the Germans sitting up and looking about him. As a precaution, Jim had tied each man's ankles. It was enough to hobble him in standing or in trying to walk, but not enough to interfere with circulation. The prisoner was evidently testing these knots. He must have grown discouraged, for, after a few minutes, he lay back in his blankets.

Thorne had shown no sign of being awake and watching this performance, but now he rose and freshened the fire. Startled and wondering how much his captor had seen, the fellow muttered something under his breath in German about an accursed dog.

So you don't like the Chief, Jim said to himself. I understood that much of your lingo, at least, though I hope you don't try using more of it on me. If you do, I'm going to have a tough time of it.

Lying down again, Jim watched the new logs catch. From the distance came the scream of some small animal brought to earth. Branches on the trees about them snapped with cold. They sounded like small, exploding firecrackers, set off without purpose or regularity. An Arctic owl whirred by. To Thorne these night noises of the north woods were as familiar as friendly voices. They were all ties binding him to this wild, lonely world that he loved, in spite of its cruelty to every living creature.

At moments like this the thought of retiring to an office job and leaving the deep snows and roaring storms forever seemed impossible. Yet he would have to do it before long. For that reason he had built his home miles across the continent in the Laurentians. In that gentler section not far from a big city, Frances and Donald were safe and warm tonight, under their own roof. Close as they were in his thoughts, his wife and son had no personal connection with this part of his life, nor did he want them to experience its bitterness and suffering.

Frances had courage and would have lived anywhere he wished, but the Northwest Territory was a hard place for a woman. It was true that at present all Donald talked about was following his father's career in service with the Royal Canadian Mounted Police. Ten years from now, though, the boy would probably seek adventure, not by dogsledge, but in the skies as so many young men were doing today.

Abruptly Jim switched his thoughts to the journey ahead and began to plan. Between here and Aklavik, he must follow the shortest route possible. Three important reasons dictated this course: food, the local accomplice, and the Government's insistence on keeping this case absolutely quiet.

His supplies were sufficient to last one man for about a week only; he now had three to feed. The dogs' meat would not last more than four days. Even with short cuts there would still be about a hundred miles to cover. Since the prisoners would have to walk, the team's speed would be slowed down to less than half its usual rate. Ordinarily he could obtain additional supplies at the first occupied cabin, but not now, for people must be avoided. Cameron Post, of course, would have to be by-passed. With the helper still unidentified, that settlement in particular remained under suspicion. This was also true, though to a lesser degree, about the occupants of lonely cabins.

For a moment he considered taking in French Pete's place. Le Brun would help him out with fresh meat and other things, and keep quiet about it. Also, this would furnish an opportunity to talk

about the young Indian, and learn what information Pete, himself, had picked up. Such a stop
might prove helpful in many ways, but common
sense warned him against it. Too many trappers
crossed the river just below the French-Canadian's winter cabin, and there was too much risk
of meeting one or more of them. At this stage of
the game he could not afford to scare off that local
man, if the fellow had quietly returned home.
Knowing that the Mounty had never gotten close
enough on the trail to see him, the accomplice
probably believed himself safe, provided the Germans did not blab.

Since the authorities demanded such secrecy
about this affair, the only thing to do was keep
clear of every man, woman, and child. The news
that Sergeant Thorne had two strangers in custody would occasion plenty of talk and questioning even in this isolated district. In time, the word
would spread; then the "fat would be in the fire"
for certain, for the authorities would empty their
wrath on the heads of the Chief Inspector at Aklavik, as well as on Sergeant Thorne.

Well, it was to be hoped luck would stay with
him by keeping people at home, Jim told himself,
and turned over for another nap.

At four o'clock the officer was up again to start

the day. After a hurried breakfast, he took stock of supplies and rationed them carefully. If they passed empty cabins, he would have to take whatever was to be found. This would break the unwritten law of the North, where a man helped himself to what was necessary for the moment but always left behind something for another's urgent need. Also, if a good opportunity offered, he would have to stop long enough to hunt down something for the dogs.

Progress was fair that day and when they passed an empty cabin near dusk, Thorne decided to stop for the night. There he found enough on the shelves to take care of a scanty supper and breakfast, but this did not help the team.

The third day he flushed some small game and brought down enough to feed the dogs for one meal. His prisoners glanced longingly at the fresh meat and muttered to themselves.

As the journey progressed, the captives, knowing that with each mile their chance to escape was growing slimmer, became more desperate. Recklessly they slogged along, whispering ever more frequently to each other and darting black scowls of hatred toward the officer and the lead dog.

In this backwoods area a dwelling was seldom to be seen. In one way this was fortunate, for

Thorne had no worry about meeting people. On the other hand, it meant fewer additional supplies than he had hoped to find.

On the fourth afternoon snow began to fall heavily. As yet, there was little wind, but when they finally stumbled on an empty cabin in which to shelter that night, Jim felt relieved. When he found several small tins of corned beef and a half tin of coffee on the otherwise empty shelves, his spirits lifted. Nothing could fully take the place of fresh meat for the dogs but the corned stuff would help out.

The Germans glanced hungrily at this find. If they expect to fill up on the beef, they were certainly doomed to disappointment, the Mounty thought to himself. In the North, a man's team was always given first consideration. Any driver with a grain of sense would tighten his own belt in order to keep his Huskies running. If the dogs stopped, that meant the end for him as well as for them.

When the prisoners discovered that only one tin of beef was to be added to the slender meal, they broke into open complaint.

Jim, who had shared equally with them all along, made only one answer, "My stomach's just as empty as yours!"

Paying no attention to his statement they continued to grumble, and the officer watched their every move. He realized that their smoldering desperation was reaching the point of explosion. There was no telling what they would attempt. Tired as he was, he forced himself to keep awake much of that night, since the Chief was beginning to tire also and might not be so alert as usual. It was a relief when the hour for rising finally came.

All night the snow had fallen and there was no promise of its stopping soon.

The shorter German's wrist injury was healing nicely and for a day or more Thorne had made him help with the preparation of food. This morning the prisoner freshened up the fire and after setting a kettle of water and the coffeepot to boil, he laid the table.

With Silver Chief as usual on guard at his heels, the other captive went out to get wood from the supply in the shed. Usually, when their hands were freed for work, the Mounty permitted neither out of his sight. This morning, though, weariness made him less careful. Without thinking, he saw the door close behind man and dog, then went about his own task of stripping the bunks. As he did this, the smell of hot coffee

He looked up just in time to dodge the kettle of water.

reached his nostrils and he felt grateful to the owner of this cabin for leaving that stimulant on the shelf. A cup was just what he needed.

Suddenly a creaking floor board close to him made Jim turn. He looked up just in time to dodge the kettle of boiling water that came hurtling through the air in his direction. With a crash, it hit the floor a few inches away. The scalding contents hissed on the cold floor boards and spattered his boots.

The next second, Thorne had the German covered and manacled. At the same instant he heard Silver Chief yelp. This was followed at once by a man's agonizing screams. Knowing that the handcuffed prisoner in the cabin could not get far even if he tried, Thorne left him where he was and made his way as swiftly as possible through the snow to the woodshed. There he found the Nazi on the floor and the dog mauling him savagely. Pulling off the Chief, Jim stooped down. Three jagged wounds marked the man's face and another, his neck, just missing the jugular vein.

Wondering exactly what had happened, Thorne looked down and saw that Silver Chief was swaying. From a wound just above the animal's right foreleg, blood was streaming. With fury burning in him, Jim helped the Chief into the cabin, laid him down carefully and temporarily stanched the injury. Catching up extra handcuffs, he pushed the other German ahead of him and went back to the man in the shed.

He now saw what he had missed on the first trip —a rusty hatchet wet with blood. Evidently the fellow had found this under the wood and had used it promptly in an attempt to kill the dog. Either his weak right arm had failed in striking or the Chief had been too quick, for the blow must have been directed at the animal's head.

Even while he noted these things, Thorne was busy unlocking and shifting handcuffs. When he finished, both of the wounded man's wrists were fastened to those of his comrade, who now stood at his head.

"Grasp his body with your hands, as I lift his feet!" Thorne said crisply.

In this fashion they carried the other into the house and laid him on a bunk. After one glance at his companion in the light, the other German paled.

Jim freed his wrists and warned, "One false move from you now and I'll shoot to kill. If there is any hot water left in the kettle pour it in a basin and bring it to me with a towel."

Obeying this order, the Nazi carried it to the bunk where his comrade lay.

"Here!" Jim called from the floor at the Chief's side.

The other's eyes widened. "But my friend will die," he began, then left the sentence unfinished.

"He'll die all right," was the answer, "but probably not here. When you've brought everything I need, you can go wash him up."

Silver Chief lay silent with eyes half closed, as his master tenderly cut off the thick, blood-stained hair, then sterilized and packed the gash. In his lifetime the dog had been injured many times but this wound was the worst he had ever received. Jim was sick at heart because he had not accompanied the Nazi and the animal to the shed. The hatchet had cut through the shoulder muscles clear to the bone. The greatest immediate danger lay in blood poisoning, for the hatchet had been old and rusted. At the moment, Thorne would willingly have given every cent he possessed for an injection of antitetanus serum. Even if the Chief would escape blood poisoning and recover, it was doubtful if the injured tendons would ever permit him to lead a team again.

Only when the wound had been neatly bandaged and taped, and the dog placed for warmth on a fur robe, did the Mounty turn his attention to the prisoner in the bunk.

Afterwards, he ate breakfast and thought grimly to himself that if he had needed the coffee before he needed it doubly now. He put on meat to cook for broth for the Chief, then with the other man as helper, fed the dogs and brought in piles of wood.

Snow was still coming down and under present circumstances there was nothing to do but stay in this cabin until the next day, at least. Whether they set out then would depend mainly on the Chief's condition.

That afternoon the dog's temperature rose, and Thorne sat beside him almost constantly, force-feeding him broth and snow water. The dog jerked restlessly in his sleep, relaxing only when his master's hand gently stroked his head.

In the bunk the wounded German moaned fitfully and complained of his companion's nursing. By evening the fellow seemed no worse. The bites he had received were ugly, but they had bled freely and infection seemed unlikely. In this case, shock had done as much damage as anything else, for in dreams the German cried out again and again about the dog.

Through the night Jim kept careful vigil beside

the Chief, dozing fitfully between times. For security he had again manacled the uninjured man, but since the combined attempt to escape had failed utterly, the fellow seemed to have become resigned to his fate.

About two in the morning, examination revealed that the dog's fever had broken and his sleep was quieter. After a moment or two, Thorne went over to his bunk and relaxed completely.

XIV

SOLVING THE PUZZLE

WHEN they rose next morning the snow had stopped falling.

Thorne went at once to Silver Chief's side and found the dog's eyes brighter and his nose cooler to the touch. His temperature was still a little higher than normal, but if it did not soar again by midmorning, serious infection was not likely to develop.

Next Jim looked at the patient in the bunk. As usual the German snarled complaints. He was badly scarred, but in general seemed no worse than on the previous day. If no change occurred in either the dog's or the man's conditions, the Mounty determined to risk continuing the journey around noon.

At this moment Jim's deepest concern was for food. Rations had been slim enough before the trouble; the extra day's delay was cutting them down to a minimum. If he had dared to leave the prisoners and the injured dog alone, he would have hunted for game. As it was, he had to stay right here to safeguard the Chief against any harm.

Fortunately the sick could be kept on limited diet. On the other hand, since they would have to ride the sledge, the pull on the team would make progress much slower. The dogs must be kept going, so they would have to be fed the bulk of what was left. Thorne and the other prisoner would be forced to live on precious little. Since one had to drive and the other to help pull, lack of food would tax their strength to the limit. When called upon to use energy in the bitter cold, the human body raged in an unceasing demand for nourishment.

About eleven o'clock, after another examination of his patients, the officer decided to push on.

In a nest of furs and blankets the sick German was set against the back rest of the sledge, and Silver Chief strapped down at his feet. When everything else was in readiness, Thorne twisted the Chief's part of the harness into a noose. Then motioning the other prisoner to the head of the team, he started to slip the noose over the man's shoulders.

For an instant trouble seemed about to break out in earnest. The German's hands and feet were both free, and at this latest indignity he blazed into violent speech.

Jim drew a revolver in warning and ordered in a voice as frigid as the air they breathed, "Get in there and pull while I drive!"

Then, with the matter attended to satisfactorily, he fell back to the side of the sledge, caught up reins and whip, and cracked out the signal to mush.

From his strapped position, Silver Chief groaned over the inability to rise and respond to his master's voice. The team surged forward and in doing so knocked down their new leader. Without help the man managed to get up on his feet and after that moved faster.

The rate of speed at which they were proceeding would not overtax his strength, for the fresh

The team knocked down their new leader.

snow made progress slow. Thorne called directions ahead and as the German broke trail, the dogs followed, straining to free their legs from the soft, clinging mass that hampered each step. Sinking deeply, the sledge runners threatened every minute to upset the load.

The Mounty plowed along, driving expertly, encouraging the team, steadying the sledge as it swayed, keeping a watchful eye on the sick dog and man. It was plain that these two did not enjoy having each other for traveling companions. The injured German seemed possessed by fear that somehow the animal at his feet would free itself and attack him again. Silver Chief did nothing to lessen this feeling of terror. When he was not napping or looking toward his master, he kept a steady, watchful gaze on this enemy. His eyes seemed to be promising further punishment at the first opportunity in the future.

About two o'clock Jim called a halt to rest the Huskies for a quarter of an hour. In that time the three men had hot tea and a little food. Silver Chief was fed broth and a few scraps of meat.

They did not stop again until nightfall. No cabin had been seen for hours and they had to camp in the open. Supper used up the last of their food, except tea, coffee, and sugar. For the dogs there remained sufficient meat for one slim meal the next day. They must reach Aklavik by the next evening—it was the only thing to do: there was no alternative.

When, after an almost superhuman effort they succeeded in doing this, Thorne turned over the prisoners, gave the team into safekeeping, and leaving Silver Chief on a bench in the outer office, went in to see the Chief Inspector.

The Old Man stared at him. "Well, Jim," he exclaimed, "they tell me you've delivered the goods as usual, but you certainly look as though you've been through a nightmare. Sit down and let's have a full report."

"If you don't mind, sir, I'd like Doc Wallace to look at the Chief first. Then, before I talk, I'd better get some grub in me. We ate our last meal twenty-four hours ago."

"Sit down in that comfortable chair," was the answer. "I'll have Wallace come right along and the restaurant can send you a good meal up here in a hurry."

The doctor appeared soon after the food was brought in. "Jim," he said, "I've been out there examining the Chief. You took good care of that injury. How did he get it?"

"From a rusty hatchet."

The physician frowned. "It's a wonder blood poisoning didn't set in."

"That's what I was afraid of," Thorne admitted, setting down his cup. "Can you tell me anything about that muscle?"

The pause following answered the question before Wallace spoke again. "I'd give something pretty if I didn't have to say this, but you've probably already guessed it. The Chief will recover. He'll even be able to run about some—but I'm very much afraid he'll never have the strength in that foreleg to lead a team again."

Jim Thorne sat in silence, with the unfinished meal before him, trying to accept this painful fact which he had suspected from the first but refused to believe.

Then he said slowly, "Can you look after him until he's well? I've got to get on the road again at once."

"Certainly, and he'll get the best care we can give him, I promise you that. Will you be back soon?"

"I hope so."

"That's all right then. He'll improve much faster if he isn't grieving for you."

"You're absolutely sure, are you, Doc?" interrupted the Chief Inspector. "Because you're telling the Royal Mounted that they've lost the best lead dog in the country."

"I realize it," was the frank reply, then turning to Jim, the doctor added, "eat the rest of that meal and get a good night's sleep before you start anywhere again." The next minute he was gone.

Shortly afterwards Thorne gave the Chief Inspector a report of all that had happened since their last meeting.

"Well, Headquarters has been notified and the plane ought to arrive in another two hours. That will take the prisoners off our hands, though I explained that this Territory has a charge of murder against them. Meanwhile, they're being questioned. I don't suppose they'll talk until confronted by their accomplice. You haven't any ideas about his identity?"

Jim told him about the young Indian. "French Pete may have found out something, and when we put two and two together we may have some real information. By the way, he hasn't sent me a letter here, has he?"

"No. Was he supposed to?" the Old Man looked a little concerned, and Thorne hastened to explain just how much he had told the French-Canadian, and the writing code they had arranged.

"What do you want done about Blaine's body?" Jim asked next.

"I'll send someone down to pick that up. You'll have enough on your hands finding that local helper. So far you've done a grand job on this assignment!"

"Thanks! I think now I'd better get back to Cameron as soon as possible."

"We'll have a fresh team and supplies ready for you tomorrow morning. In the meantime do what Wallace suggested—sleep and eat!" He held out his hand. "I'm sorry about your dog, Jim, I know what he means to you."

After leaving the office, Thorne spent a few minutes with Silver Chief. Then he took a steaming hot bath and fell into bed.

The next thing he knew, someone was knocking on his door to say that everything was ready whenever he wished to go. He ate breakfast, dashed off a note to his family, and stopped in once more to see the Chief before starting out.

The new team proved strong and fresh. Since their load was light, Thorne drove most of the way sitting down. When he finally arrived at Cameron he felt more rested than in many days. He headed straight for the Trading Post. There he would learn promptly if anyone had stumbled across the cabin sheltering Blaine's body, or if Sergeant Thorne had been seen traveling with two men in custody.

His unexpected appearance surprised everyone. He exchanged greetings with Mac, Hughes, and several other men, then swung Pat up in his arms.

"Sergeant Jim, is the Chief outside?" she asked in the next breath.

"I left the Chief and the other dogs with friends for a rest, and drove a whole new team down here."

The child showed her disappointment. Then she went on, "My father hasn't come yet. Did you see him?"

"Yes, I saw him," the Mounty told her, wincing inwardly. "Now you run along for a minute and let me talk with Uncle Mac."

One thing was sure. No one present knew about Blaine. He had watched their faces as the child mentioned her father, and expressions had remained unchanged. He walked with MacDonald to the rear of the room.

"Lately I've been wishing you were around, Jim," Mac began, "but I certainly never expected to see you so soon."

"Something doing?"

"Nothin' you can really lay your hands on."
The trader stopped to light his pipe. After several puffs he went on, "I've a feelin' there's trouble
brewin' between one of the Indians and a white
man, and you never know where that's going to
lead. Even when it's just a matter of a stolen fox-
skin, the Indians can stir up a pretty big rumpus.
In the case of a girl . . ." he shook his head.

"Suppose you start at the beginning, Mac."

MacDonald told him about the young Indian's
visit to the store. "Since then," he continued,
"there have been rumors goin' around. When
white men or breeds spread tales, I don't take
much stock in them, but these seem to have come
from Indians."

"Where's this fellow live?"

The trader described the location of the village. "You've been there, haven't you?"

Jim nodded. "What's he look like?"

After supplying this information, Mac said,
"I hope what I've told you won't get him into
trouble. Swift-as-Wind has always been a decent
young fellow and I have the feelin' some white
man's served him a dirty trick."

"Swift-as-Wind—is that his name?"

"It's what most of them call him. He's the fastest runner in this section."

"I agree with you it might bear looking into, particularly if he's always behaved himself. Maybe we can save him from doing something rash."

"Are you opening up the police cabin?"

"No, I'm making another patrol."

"Well, stay here for supper and the night."

"I'd like to, but I think I'll keep going this afternoon. If nothing happens I'll be back soon."

Hughes walked up. "Sergeant, did you know Blaine hadn't come yet?"

"So Pat said," Jim answered, then said, "so long." He stopped to talk for a few minutes with the little girl, and promising to come again soon went outside.

Cutting through the bush toward French Pete's, Thorne thought of the young Indian, Swift-as-Wind. So that was the fellow's name, and that was why he had been able to cut through woods and catch up with Thorne's sledge that morning more than two weeks ago. Being the fastest runner in the district also explained how he could have trailed the hated white man and his two passengers.

After arriving at Le Brun's, the Mounty talked at length with the trapper. Seriously, he considered Pete's two suspects, the Swede and French Charlie.

Abruptly he asked, "Do you know a young Indian called Swift-as-Wind?"

"Yes, his lines cross mine."

"What kind of fellow is he?"

"A good Indian, dat one!"

"Has he had any trouble with a white man, do you know?"

Le Brun looked surprised. "I 'ave not 'ear." He seemed trying to recall a memory. "Now, I know!" he exclaimed. "Sarzhan', in dat village dere is trouble, but Indian trouble—ol' one an' young one."

"Who told you?"

"A breed."

"Who is the woman French Charlie's marrying?"

"He don' tell."

"White or Indian?"

Pete shrugged his shoulders expressively in ignorance.

"And you've never heard of any trouble between Swift-as-Wind and either the Swede, or Charlie?"

"Non, Sarzhan'."

"Well, Pete, the fact remains that Swift-as-Wind has a grudge against some white man and a girl is mixed up with it all."

The French-Canadian's eyes lighted suddenly. "So-o! You believe, Sarzhan', dat is girl Charlie marry?"

"Perhaps! Let's suppose Swift-as-Wind wants to marry a maiden in his village. A white man wishes to marry the same girl. Perhaps he drives a better bargain with the father than Swift-as-Wind can do and is promised the maid. This makes the young brave angry with both the father and the white man. In earlier days, he would have had the white man's scalp, but now if he uses violence the white man's law will kill him. Then luck comes his way. He catches his enemy doing something queer. Just about that time a white policeman happens along. Swift-as-Wind slips through the woods secretly, heads off the policeman, and gives him this information. Then the youth waits for something to happen. Nothing does. His enemy is as free as ever. The policeman does not return. So Swift-as-Wind runs wild. He begins to quarrel with other white men, and to talk against them to the young Indians of his village—" Thorne stopped abruptly, then finished, "And here we are!"

Pete, who had been listening with the deepest interest and nodding agreement to most details, now raised one objection, "But, Sarzhan', how

could Charlie offair more dan brave did, unless—"

"Unless he had suddenly found some money,"
Thorne said, "and that's what I have to discover.
You said that the Indian's lines cross yours, Pete.
When does he usually work them?"

"Early."

"And you?"

" 'Bout same time."

"I'll go down there with you in the morning,
then part company. I want to see him alone."

XV

"BY THIS LAW I SWEAR!"

EARLY the following morning the two men
set out on foot for the place where they were
likely to meet Swift-as-Wind. Pete took care of
his traps in that vicinity, then moved on his way
swiftly. Jim stationed himself behind a clump of
trees to wait. Shortly afterwards the Indian approached. If he had not been lost in unhappy
thought, he would have become aware of Thorne's
presence earlier.

When the youth was within ten yards, Jim

178

stepped out and said softly, "Swift-as-Wind, I want to talk to you alone." Adding helpful gestures, he slowly repeated this statement.

Motionless, the Indian stood where he was as if poised for immediate flight. For an instant the black eyes flickered in recognition, then the lids shuttered them. His lips made no sound, but the officer knew that the other was now as alert as a wild animal to any move that might be made. The next minute the young man turned and slipped like a shadow into the deeper woods.

Thorne followed. When they had arrived at a hidden spot where other trackers were unlikely to come, Swift-as-Wind stopped and facing about, spoke for the first time, "What policeman want?"

"To help you," Jim said first in English, then in the other's own tongue.

There now began for the second time between these two a conversation that was a mixture of simple English and Indian dialect. The youth made it clear that he wanted no help from anyone, particularly a white man.

With a nod of understanding, Thorne said, "One white man your enemy; other white men your friends."

The youth contradicted stubbornly. He had no interest in white men, friends, or enemies.

"But you told me of the three white men going south," the Mounty put into the broken speech.

This was received in silence. Then Swift-as-Wind muttered something about working his lines. He took a step forward restlessly.

He's nervous, Jim thought to himself, knowing that Indians could stand still indefinitely. If anything were to be accomplished by this conversation, now was the time to get tough.

"You want the driver to marry the maiden?" he asked.

The young man's expression remained as wooden as before but for a second his right hand twitched. In the next breath words poured from his lips.

Able to understand only a part of this, Jim let the speech run its course before replying. "I can help you. What is that driver's name?"

Silence followed. Then, as if the words were being torn from him, the Indian explained that doing what the policeman asked would not help. Already there had been trouble with the maiden's father. This would make more. The old man would be very angry. If his daughter did not marry the white man, he would give her to someone else, never to Swift-as-Wind himself.

"Her father will not know. If you tell me your enemy's name, it shall be a secret between you and me," came the promise.

"By what law will the policeman swear?"

Jim pushed aside his parka and pointed to the badge on his tunic. Realizing how seriously Indians thought of symbols, he said in a solemn voice, "By this law, the high law of the white man, I swear your people shall not know. This law will punish your enemy. You can go back to your village and live at peace."

There was no further hesitation. The next instant he had the information that French Charlie was the man he sought, and that Charlie had been at home for several days.

As on the previous occasion, the young Indian disappeared without another word, and Thorne made his way thoughtfully back to French Pete's where he had left his team.

The job now was to pin the guilt on Charlie. There was no material evidence to connect him with the Germans. Trappers came and went through the snows about their work and no one checked their movements. This was particularly true of the man in question, whose recent absences from the trap lines would mean to his neighbors only that he had lazily remained in his cabin while others worked. Apparently no one had seen him with strangers except the young Indian who was naturally interested in everything his rival did. For that matter, as far as strangers were concerned, it was as though they had never been, as far as the trappers were interested. True, there had been boot tracks, but the men who had made them seemed to have become invisible as they passed through the Cameron district. Jim would certainly be interested in knowing what Headquarters had learned about the Nazis' progress in this particular section.

There was no evidence against Charlie; there was also no witness, now that Jim had sworn to keep the Indian's name secret. Under these circumstances the guilty man would have to be caught somehow in the net of his own speech. If this could be done, again a witness would be needed to legalize the testimony. Pete, who already knew more than anyone else, was the logical man to help, but Thorne hesitated to ask one French-Canadian to testify against another even though the two had little to do with each other. Also, if Pete did so, he would at once become an object of suspicion in the neighborhood. The average man trusted the law, but distrusted any civilian who worked with it.

Well, the cloud of suspicion had finally been lifted from the other men around here. As for the one to help from now on—MacDonald was the best choice, for in his position as Post trader he represented the Government and no one would criticize his helping the police catch a criminal.

By this time Jim had reached Le Brun's. He sat down and carefully worded a note thanking and complimenting the trapper for his efforts. Next, he added the warning that the entire affair, no matter what might happen, must never be mentioned. When finished, the note was read for a second time. Then, confident that the wording would make it a puzzle to anyone but Pete, he placed it on the table and set an iron pot on top of it.

Later the Mounty drove at a leisurely pace up the main trail toward Cameron Village. For the rest of the day idleness faced him. Not until dusk could he and Mac set out, for no suspicions must be aroused.

Halfway to the settlement, Jim became aware that another team was hurriedly overtaking his. He pulled aside to let it pass.

The driver did so, then slowed down to a full stop and shouted, "Jim, where in the dickens did you come from? And where's the Chief?"

Then before an answer could be made, the speaker ran on in his usual manner, "When I saw you last you were acting sort of queer. I knew you were on the hunt for somebody and I hope you got him. Say, you haven't told me yet where the Chief is!"

Jim grinned at Postman Andrews. Then, with sudden inspiration, he said, "Soapy, you're just the man I wanted to see. I've got a job on my hands and I need help. You couldn't have come at a better time."

"I'll help you all right, but you still haven't told me about the dog. I want to know about him before you go any further."

"I left him and the team at Aklavik to rest up. They'd had a long, hard run and I was anxious to get back here."

"Don't tell me they're having some excitement in Cameron!"

"Well, Cameron doesn't know it yet, and that's where you come in."

"Who is it and what's the charge?"

"French Charlie," Thorne said in a low voice. "The charge—accomplice in a murder."

"Bury me in a snowdrift," Soapy murmured. "That's one of the laziest white men alive. I didn't suppose he had energy enough to get into any trouble, let alone that kind. Now what do you want me to do?"

"Be at French Pete's soon after dusk. Do you suppose you can think up a good excuse for leaving Mac's at that time?"

"I'll just say I can't spend the night and he'll have to get the mail ready early. By the way, where will we sleep?"

"If the plan works, I'd like to push right on. I want to get him to Aklavik as fast as possible."

Andrews sighed. "Well, I guess I'm not too old to lose one night's rest," he said. "The team can lie around all day at Mac's and maybe I'll do some of that myself. Is little Pat still staying with them, or is her father at Cameron?"

Now what made him ask that last? Jim thought silently as he answered, "She's with Mac and Danny."

"You know," Soapy hurried to add, "I have a letter for Blaine. I stopped by his place but couldn't find a soul to leave it with. Looked like something queer had been going on there. Things were in an awful mess, and Blaine has always kept his place neat as a pin. Maybe not having his wife around is making him careless."

"Well, men get that way," Thorne replied carefully. "It might be better not to mention that to anyone at Cameron. If Danny hears Blaine has left home, he's going to worry his head off. The old fellow's crazy about the youngster, and the thought of her leaving is pretty hard on him."

"Glad you reminded me to keep my mouth shut. She's certainly one nice little girl. You know, Jim, most people around here think Blaine's a queer cuss, but he's got a lot of good in him."

The Mounty nodded slowly in agreement, then hastened to add, "Now don't forget! It's French Pete's after dusk, and you're supposed to be hurrying back to Aklavik with the post."

"I understand. So long!" With a crack of his whip Soapy swung along toward Cameron.

Thorne turned back to Le Brun's. The accident of Soapy's arrival just then was the best thing that could have happened. Now no local citizen need be connected with the affair. The postman was not only a Government employee; he could help and be out of the section before any news broke. Andrews had only one fault—he sometimes talked too freely, but when ordered to keep a secret, he could do it as well as anyone.

Already Thorne was shaping in his mind a plan for tricking the guilty man, provided the fellow *was* guilty. After all he had only the Indian's word to that effect. If Swift-as-Wind had lied to get rid of the officer, Charlie, being innocent, would not walk into the trap. Then the whole scheme would blow up. However, the risk had to be made.

Pete had not yet reached home when Thorne returned for the second time. The Mounty ate lunch, tore up the note he had left, and lay down for a nap. Later when the trapper came in, they had an early supper and a long farewell conversation in which Thorne told of his arrangement with the postman.

At the appointed time Andrews drove up. His team was put under shelter at the French-Canadian's and he boarded Thorne's sledge. He was equipped with a flashlight, paper, and pencils. About fifty yards from Charlie's the sledge halted to let him off, and Thorne drove up, knocked, and was admitted. Soapy crept up to the door a few minutes later to listen.

When Charlie recognized his guest, he looked disturbed. Then, getting hold of himself, he forced a smile and said, "Well, Sergeant, you're on patrol later than usual. Is there something I can do for you?"

Sitting down, Thorne threw back his parka.

"Just checking up on a few things, Charlie," he replied and wondered at the difference between this French-Canadian's speech and Pete's.

Maybe the fellow's parents had brought him to Canada earlier. Certainly he had attended Canadian schools to speak English this well.

"Have you had a good season?"

"Fair."

"Everybody around here seems to be making money," Thorne continued pleasantly. "You must have more than most."

"Me, Sergeant?" Charlie said as if in pained surprise, then shook his head. "I'm afraid I'm not a very good trapper. I do not catch as many as my neighbors, so I am always poor."

The Mounty relaxed in the chair. "I did not mean money for furs, but what the Germans paid you for your help," he explained.

Charlie's fat face became ashen. Then he managed to say slowly between dry lips, "Germans? What Germans, Sergeant?"

Well, the Indian didn't lie, Thorne told himself —he's guilty all right. "I mean the two Germans you took to Blaine's cabin," he went on aloud, as smoothly as if they were discussing the weather. "They should have paid a good deal for your services."

"They lie! They lie!" Charlie shouted.

Charlie swallowed and tried to smile again. "You must have made a mistake, Sergeant. I know no Germans, and where did you say it was they were taken?"

The officer crossed his knees, but his right hand slid down to his belt. Then he asked, "Did you really think Blaine would not tell, Charlie?"

The other's jaw sagged. "But Blaine is dead," he exclaimed. "I saw him fall!" Realizing what he had said, Charlie stood as if paralyzed by terror.

Thorne pressed his advantage swiftly home. "And if he did not die? And if he and the two Germans all say you shot him, what then?"

"They lie! They lie!" Charlie shouted in a frenzy. "I told them not to kill the prospector. I knew you would find his body on the trail. They said they would take care of you. At the next woods, we would make two trails. If you followed them, they would be waiting. If you followed me, they would shoot you when you drove past. They missed you. I saw you turn back. I hurried on." He stopped abruptly, shaking from head to foot.

"You knew they were enemy Germans, why did you help them?"

"I did not care what they were. I needed money," was the sullen answer.

Covering him with a revolver, Thorne rose, crossed the room, and clicking handcuffs on the guilty man, said formally, "I arrest you under the Law of Canada: first, for giving aid to the enemy; second, as an accomplice in the murder of Frank Blaine."

"But Blaine—if he talked . . ." Charlie objected, snatching at hope.

"Frank Blaine is dead and for no reason," Jim answered sharply.

The prisoner's little pig eyes narrowed and stared venomously at his captor. "You tricked me, Policeman," he shot out. "Now I will trick you. I will tell the Government all you say is a lie. You cannot prove me guilty."

"Andrews," the officer called out, "you can come in now."

When Soapy entered the room, Charlie saw his last hope fade.

"Did you get it all down?" Jim asked.

"Yes, though my fingers were getting stiff near the end."

"Better sign it and give it to me, now."

Soapy did so, and the officer carefully read the account of his recent conversation with French Charlie. "That's just what I wanted. Thanks. As soon as you get warmed up, we'll start."

Turning to the prisoner, Thorne helped him get the things he needed for the journey and bank the fire so it would gradually die away and cause no trouble. Blowing out the light and grasping his prisoner firmly by the arm, he led the party into the bitter, frozen silence of the northern night.

XVI

PAT BLAINE FINDS A HAVEN

THE two sledges made steady progress through the night. Each of the three men was lost in his own thoughts. The prisoner was overcome by despair. Postman Andrews felt deeply shocked by the news of Frank Blaine's murder and the fact that strange Germans were guilty of the crime. Thorne's mind busied itself with many things: getting the captive safely to Aklavik; guessing what the court would do with the three men involved; and wondering how to arrange for small Pat Blaine's future.

The trip itself was uneventful. Andrews' team was now a little better than the Mounty's; the sledges were about equally loaded. The postman made as usual few stops on his return trip, and they managed to keep together until they finally reached their destination.

In front of the Post Office the two men parted. Keeping his prisoner covered, Jim stepped aside for a final word with Andrews.

"Since both Blaine and Charlie have now disappeared from the Cameron district, there is bound to be a lot of talk. The less said the better," he cautioned. "If people can think that Blaine died from an accident, that will be fine. They can believe what they want about Charlie; he wasn't very popular anyway. One thing is extremely important; you know absolutely nothing about any Germans. If the Government would let me do so, I'd tell you the whole story. As things are, we'll have to let the Germans vanish into thin air."

"I'm willing to keep quiet, Jim," Andrews said, "but of course the story of the trial is going to get back to Cameron after a while."

"I doubt it. This affair, as far as I can see, is going to die in Government files."

"So, it's like that! Well, count on me to be mum. I hope whoever killed Blaine'll get what he deserves for it. Makes it tough on little Pat."

"They'll get what they deserve, all right—you needn't worry about that. Thanks again for your help!" Thorne shook hands, then drove on to the police building.

There he promptly handed over his prisoner and walked in to make his report.

"You look better, Jim, than you did the other day," the Chief Inspector said in greeting. "Now let's hear all about it. Before you commence, though, I'd better tell you that Doc Wallace says that dog of yours is coming along fine."

Thorne's eyes lighted. "That's good. When I get through here, I'll look him over myself," he answered.

When all the details of this man hunt had been fully discussed, Jim asked, "Did Headquarters get a confession of any sort?"

"Only after a good deal of hard work. It was the taller fellow who broke down. His nerves must have been shattered by what Silver Chief did to him. They were slick birds, though. The thing that particularly interested me was where they got their money. You remember in that diary they seemed able to pay for things."

Thorne nodded.

"They broke into a store in the first town they reached after escaping," the other went on, "and got away with everything in the cash box and two revolvers and cartridges, as well. There had already been two robberies in that town just before they arrived, so the local police lumped them all together, never dreaming that the third theft had been committed by complete strangers. Accordingly, Headquarters skipped this clue altogether."

"But that diary never mentioned lack of food, either," puzzled Jim. "When did they strike their first real snag—in the deep snows?"

"Right. They knew nothing about the need for snowshoes and actually tried to proceed in ordinary footwear. At this point their confession became somewhat hazy. They got as far as Cameron River and there, when they had just about reached the end of their strength, the trapper happened along. Only when they had promised him most of their money would he agree to help. He didn't dare to keep them around Cameron, so he took them to Blaine's lonely cabin. The plan was for them to hide out until they were stronger, then make a break for the west coast. The trapper knew that you were in Cameron

District and he was to be paid more money for keeping them informed of your movements. When he got wind of your going to Blaine's, he hurried up there. You know the rest."

"Which one shot Blaine?"

"The taller. He seemed very proud of his marksmanship. Said he never needed but one cartridge to get any man."

"Well, he missed me, though I'll agree it was much too close for comfort."

"Where are you going from here, Jim?"

"Back to Cameron first, then home if you don't need me. Something's got to be arranged about Blaine's little daughter." Thorne explained his reasons for feeling responsible in this case, and added, "If I can borrow a lead dog, I'll take my own Huskies back this trip. The Chief, I hope, can go along as passenger."

"That means you'll go straight home from Cameron, instead of coming here again?"

Jim nodded. "If you agree."

"When are you starting?"

"There's no mad rush this time. Tomorrow forenoon, I suppose."

"Well, pick the dog you want and be sure to come in before you go! I want to see you again." The Chief Inspector's eyes twinkled, then he said soberly, "My, Jim, I wish you were ten years younger again. Well, you've certainly earned an easier job than sticking to the trail."

Thorne looked puzzled. "Does this mean the Royal Mounted is really through with me?"

"Not entirely," the Old Man answered, but refused to say anything more, and Jim took his departure.

Sometimes, lately, the Chief Inspector seemed to be showing his years, Jim thought as he headed for Doctor Wallace's quarters. Then he shrugged the thought off.

As soon as he opened Doc's door, his big, gray friend and companion of many a lonely hour tried to leap all over him, almost opening his nearly healed wound in the mad excitement of seeing his master again. Forcing him down, Thorne sat beside the Chief and rubbed his head until he had quieted.

"We've had to force-feed him, Jim, ever since you left," Wallace said. "That never has as good results as a normal appetite does. Still, he has gotten along pretty well."

"Think I can take him along with me to Cameron tomorrow as a passenger?"

"I don't see why not. He'll continue improving twice as fast if he's with you."

"Well, Old Fellow," Thorne promised, turning to the dog, "you can count on starting out in the morning."

After the doctor had given him medicine and directions for massaging the dog's injured muscles, Jim left to attend to personal affairs. He wrote a long letter to his wife, telling her when he hoped to reach home, then renewed acquaintance with a number of old friends.

He slept later than usual the following morning. When his team was ready and Silver Chief was strapped on the sledge again, he drove over to see the Chief Inspector.

To his astonishment, the Old Man looked up as he entered and said, "Good morning, Inspector, are you on your way?"

Thorne stared for a second, then supposing that this had been just a slip of the tongue, replied that he was.

"You said you wanted to see me again, sir," he suggested.

"Yes, there's a telegram here for you to read. It came just a little while ago." He pushed it over to Thorne.

Jim picked up the paper, wondering if it were bad news from home, and glanced at the contents hurriedly. More slowly, he read it a second time.

He could not believe his eyes. The words informed him that his rank was now that of Inspector and that he had been appointed head of the Force in a city not far from his home.

"Well, Inspector, what do you think of it?" the Old Man said with a chuckle in his voice.

"I haven't got my breath yet," Thorne answered. "Give me a little time."

"You know in this service promotions come slowly sometimes," the Chief Inspector remarked. "You've deserved another for a good while. Ottawa gave the police authorities a push in your case, and I suggested the desk job. You're worth too much to the Royal Mounted to slip out and join up with some business firm."

"Well, this has been my life, and I never have wanted to go into business, though there have been several good offers. Since I'd have to withdraw from active service soon, I'd rather have a position of this sort than I would anything else."

"I knew that, Jim, and while I won't be able to count on you in future emergencies, I'm glad for you just the same."

Other members of the Force now came in to offer congratulations, and Thorne set off for Cameron amid a flurry of good wishes.

In good time he reached his destination. At the Post he found to his satisfaction that Mac, Hughes, and Pat were alone.

After greeting them he said, "Bill, can you put me up for the night?"

"Of course."

"Then, Danny, if you'll help me carry the Chief inside, we'll make him comfortable first."

"Is the Chief sick, Sergeant Jim?" Pat asked in dismay.

"No, something happened to a foreleg, but he's getting along fine now."

Silver Chief was carried in and placed on a rug at one side of the store. Pat immediately settled herself beside the dog and stayed there petting him most of the day.

That night when the little girl was asleep and the three men once more alone, Thorne informed the others of Blaine's death.

Mac received the news in stunned silence, but Hughes blurted out, "How did it happen, Sergeant?"

"He got badly hurt, Danny, and I found his body."

MacDonald said slowly, "That makes it pretty hard for the young one; now she has neither parent left."

Pat settled herself beside the dog.

"Do you know whether she has any relatives outside, Mac?" the Mounty asked.

"I'm afraid not, Jim. Blaine told me when his wife died that they were alone in the world."

Danny looked bleak. "If I hadn't been such a danged fool an' wasted my money, I'd have some now an' I'd adopt her."

"Money's only a small part of it, Danny," Bill told him. "I guess Jim's got some ideas about her."

"Well," admitted Thorne, "Blaine left a note asking me to see that she was looked out for, and I'm trying to make up my mind what's best."

"I suppose two old bachelors wouldn't make the wisest guardians for her," the trader said thoughtfully, "otherwise I'd ask you to let Hughes and me have her."

Danny was leaning forward with excitement but for once he had nothing to say.

"I don't believe she'll find anyone to think more of her than you two do. If you really want the responsibility, I've a proposition. Frances wrote me months ago to bring the child home if Blaine agreed. I wouldn't hear of that, at the time, and now I know Blaine wouldn't have either. He was more interested in Pat than we knew. In his note he insisted that his claim was valuable and the child must benefit from it. If you two could arrange to have that looked after, and worked if it's worth anything, that would take care of the first problem."

"All right, consider it scratched off," Mac offered. "Danny and I'll take over there. If it's good, we'll pay somebody to do the work and once in a while we can go supervise. What's next?"

"She's got to have the schooling and companions her mother wanted for her."

"But she can't get them here," Danny replied unhappily.

"No; there's where Frances and I come in. If you two want to adopt her legally, she can live with us in the school year and come home to you in the summers."

Danny's eyes were shining. "And she'd really be ours then?"

He got up suddenly, strode quickly over to the stove, and stuffed it full of wood with unusual vigor.

"Since you've your own family to look out for, Jim," Mac broke in, "we'll pay her expenses. I've got something salted down, you know, and I'd rather spend it this way than any other. If you and your wife are willing to have the responsibility of another young one in your home, you'll be doing more than your share."

For another hour they continued to discuss the matter in detail. Silver Chief lay on the rug where his master had ordered him to stay and watched the men between dozes. The injury no longer pained him, but he was still weak and quite content to lie still. So long as he could see Thorne and listen to his voice, the dog was at peace.

The next morning after breakfast, Jim took Pat off by herself and asked, "Young lady, how would you like to go to my home for a visit?"

The child looked up at him. "Would the Chief go along?" she wanted to know.

Thorne smiled. "Yes, indeed. I wouldn't dare to go home without him."

"Will we get back before my father comes?"

Thorne smoothed her hair. "Pat, your father has gone away and I'm afraid he won't be back."

"You mean like my mother?"

"Yes, so Uncle Mac and Uncle Danny and I want you to be our little girl."

Pat said nothing. She seemed to be trying hard to understand all of this strange news.

To distract her attention Jim said, "If you'll get your things together I think we'll start on our trip this morning."

"But what about Uncle Danny and Uncle Mac?"

"You'll come back here to see them later on. Come on now, like a good girl, and get ready."

By noon the party was ready to start. Pat and the Chief were warmly and comfortably settled on the sledge.

Saying good-by to the two men, the Mounty promised, "I'll drop you a line from the railroad center, if I have time after shipping the Huskies back to Aklavik and getting the Chief settled in the baggage car on our train."

"I suppose your address hasn't changed," Mac said.

"Not for a time at least," was the reply. "You'd better direct it, 'Inspector,' instead of 'Sergeant,' though."

Both men showed their surprise. "And here I've been calling you 'Sergeant' ever since you came in yesterday," Danny exclaimed. "Why didn't you tell us?"

"Congratulations, Inspector!" added the trader. "If anybody was ever due a promotion, you were, Jim."

Flushing, Thorne smiled in appreciation. Without further comment he stepped on the runners and waved a farewell. Behind him the two men stood on the steps of the Trading Post and watched with deep concern while the sledge carrying Pat Blaine toward a new life disappeared gradually from view.

Responding to their master's commands, the team of Huskies raced across the plain. As the winter wore on and the year neared springtime, the hours of light increased in number and power. Today the gray mist seemed to glint with the hidden promise of brighter days to come.

For Jim Thorne the weather this noontide seemed to symbolize his own feelings about the future. His promotion from Sergeant to Inspector had come as a deep surprise. At once it had put an end to the torment of making a decision about the rest of his career. As head of the Force in the city to which he had been assigned, he would continue with the Royal Mounted. There would be times, no doubt, when the lure of the deep snows would call to him, and the thought of running beside a dog team would make the blood hammer in his ears. Such moments would pass, though, and he would be satisfied to share in spirit the danger and thrill of the jobs he assigned his men. And, for the first time since he joined the Force, he would have the chance to enjoy his home and the companionship of his wife and child.

Glancing down at the two occupants of the

sledge, Jim wondered what was passing through Pat Blaine's young mind. Except for moments of interest in the trail ahead, the child's attention was centered in the dog strapped at her feet. It was almost as if, in the midst of changes, Pat found Silver Chief the firmest, steadiest thing in her world.

From time to time the Chief eyed little Pat protectingly, but for the most part his deep, loving gaze settled on Thorne. Why his master was making him ride the sledge again while a strange Husky led the team was more than the great wolfdog could understand. Something was wrong with one of his legs, but even so, given the chance, he would soon make the stranger realize who was the real leader of this team. Aside from this matter, nothing troubled his magnificent head.

Silver Chief had no way of knowing that the rest of his life would be spent in the security of his master's home. There, thought and affection would be lavished on him. Even if he had understood that the days of the long treks were over, he would not have cared. He was concerned with one thing only—to be with the man who was driving this team. For the sake of Jim Thorne's companionship, the dog would willingly endure hunger, hardship, suffering, and death. Separation from his master was the only thing he feared. At present they were together, and that was enough. Under the straps he wriggled to stretch his great gray body, then bent his muzzle forward to lick at the wound in his chest. When this had been done to his satisfaction, he closed his eyes, after another glance at Thorne, and relaxed in complete contentment.

The End